THE
BRINDLE

J. Jennings Melton

J. Jennings Melton
Visit my website at www.JJenningsMelton.com

Printed in the United States of America

US Copyright Office Registration Number TXu 2-065-270 August 16, 2017

The Writers Guild of America, East Inc. Registration Number I303814 August 16, 2017

First Printing: March 2018
CreateSpace, a DBA of On-Demand Publishing, LLC.

ISBN-13 978-0-6920713-1-1

* * *

To the Reader:

This novel is an adaptation of a screenplay which I wrote with the same title. I acknowledge that readers will take from this story that which they most relate with, as is the case with any book, movie, song, etc., but please keep in mind that "The Brindle" is the story of a dog that was made to fight and not a tale of dog fighting.

When one writes about subject matter our society labels "taboo" there will always be criticism from people who cannot see the forest for the trees. "The Brindle" is not merely a tale told for entertainment purpose, it is also meant to shed light on two very real problems. Autism and Animal Abuse and the two come to a crossroad in that animals, dogs, have been shown to improve the disposition of Autistic persons significantly.

I attempted to write a story that was informative, entertaining, eye opening and graphic enough to reveal the plight of abused animals while at the same time trying to soften the subject matter enough to remain appropriate for younger audiences. It was a real juggling act, and I sincerely hope that I did not drop the ball.

If at the end of the book my readers feel a bit more informed, a little more determined to help an abused animal or a desire to learn more about Autism, and of course entertained, then I have indeed succeeded as an author, and that is the best a writer can hope for.

J. Jennings Melton

"THE BRINDLE"
INTRODUCTION

There are a few crimes as heinous as that of dog fighting – child abuse being the human equivalent. A dog, like a child, is innocent and dependent, its very nature is to love and trust its custodian unconditionally. For that trust to be so callously abused for the sake of profit and entertainment is as evil an action as man has ever committed.

The life of a fighting dog, if it can, in fact, be called a life, is one of such unimaginable horrors. He is bred solely for the sake of battle. His days, from birth to death, will be filled with unrelenting torment. Training so brutal that some dogs die from rigors of the routines alone.

Pain, loneliness, and violence are all a part of each day's exercise until it's taken for granted, by the animal, that the very definition of life and living is misery. No love, no kindness, his life is one of blood and war.

If lucky, he will lose early and die young because to win is to survive and, in his world,, survival means further anguish, to be used again and again, only to meet the same inevitable end.

The day will come, sooner or later, when he is unable to rise, no longer able to win and his misery will end by way of a bullet, strangulation, or drowning.

An entire life, from womb to shallow grave, having never known the feeling of love or the meaning of joy, could any creature emerge from such an environment, not having become a monster?

FORWARD

His opponent is ferocious, larger, stronger, and out of control with blood lust. The monster quivers, muscles spasm, as he strains the chain that binds him.

Across the pit, he stands calm and collected. Twenty pounds lighter the dog stares across at his massive foe, though smaller, his short hair seems stretched like latex over the sinewy muscles that ripple beneath his multicolored coat. Twenty pounds lighter, but every ounce of it the perfect material which makes him the best the old man has ever made.

Since his teeth broke through the gums, he has been trained...baptized in blood for this sole purpose...created for this one thing. Fear and panic, feelings as alien to him as joy and kindness. There is a difference between him and his opponent, more than just size and mentality, for he is calculating, imaginative and even analytical.

The collars are broken, his large enemy rushes forward, left paw digging deep into the Georgia dirt, his massive head lolling in a circular motion as he advances.

Just before the monster arrives, he shifts his weight, in a feint, to the beast's right. The brute takes the bait and swings his massive head to attack the smaller dog.

A blur of motion moves to his left followed instantly by a terrible pressure in his neck. The brute struggles to defend himself, but like most of the men witnessing this slaughter, he does not know he is the underdog.

The left paw digging deeper than the right showed his smaller, brilliant, opponent that the beast favors his left paw and so counter attacking to his right side is what the monster was most comfortable with. The lolling motion of the beast's head betrays hip dysplasia, a condition that makes turning side to side slow and painful.

The smaller animal sinks his teeth into the neck of the larger dog and throws a paw over his foe's back as he begins twisting his neck, which pulls the monster's head upward and back, further and further, before a yipe escapes the beast's now gaping mouth.

The head is pulled back further still, as he twists his own head more until the big black body of his foe shudders and a loud pop is heard that silences the crowd. The limp body collapses to the dirt floor as he scans the men's shocked faces to find the one that does not look at all surprised.

The old man nods his head, and it is the one single gesture that he has come to covet more than anything in his life, for in that gesture there is a magic which stirs within him something he cannot comprehend – a feeling which repels the torment of living for a fraction of a moment and in these moments the hate he feels for the old man fades...for a fleeting moment.

He does not understand why he must fight and kill as he looks down at the lifeless form at his paws but knows to do otherwise would mean to end up, himself, at the paws of another. He knows nothing of his latest foe, had never seen him before but his own instincts to survive are powerful, and so he will kill if he must.

There is another difference between him and the rest, something that he possesses that even the men around the pit, and certainly the old man, lack.

As the body of the fallen is dragged away, he feels a pang within his broad chest. A feeling he cannot understand or control; pity, sadness. It fades as the collar is clasped roughly around the thick callous around his neck and is led back through the crowd but always it lingers, joining the others to come in waves to haunt him at night as he sleeps.

All their faces, flashing back, so many he has begun to forget the one face he longs to remember, and with each new face hers fades more and more.

CHAPTER 1

Quantico, Virginia four years earlier.

Before he enters the gymnasium, John Ryan knows who and what they are. He hasn't looked at their files, doesn't know their history, stories, names or races for that matter, but he knows that each will have a chip on their shoulder and that all eight, the five men and three women, are over achievers.

He has been training up-and-coming-agents hand-to-hand combat for ten years. Every year he is given the cream of the crop of the rookie class to show their limits and bring them down a peg. He knows his course is famous for its brutality and for having never passed a female cadet.

As he walks through the door, he locates the eight rookies who all straighten up instantly. Like each class before them, they stand shoulder to shoulder in agency issued sweat outfits. In the corner, where the workout equipment is, groups of the usual loiter around to witness the newbie's first day. Ryan enjoys putting on a show and as he closes in on his prey, he knows who will pass and who will fail.

The three women, one black, one white and one brown will be gone within a couple of days but the five men, Ryan notes, all have that look.

He dismisses the females instantly and concentrates on the eyes of the men, each have the look of battle hardened warriors. He holds back a smile and restrains his excitement. To have five real soldiers like these young men in one class...he can hardly contain himself.

"I'll make this quick and to the point." Ryan walks from one end of the line of cadets to the other only out of habit, but he can't wait to concentrate his time where it counts and dismiss these women, although the Mexican broad is completely doable.

"I know you have all scored outstanding in marksmanship, surveillance, interrogation, and written exams but all of that means exactly squat in this class. There are no weapons, equipment or partners here, in this class you rely on your brains, body, and instincts. Here only the best men get passing grades."

Ryan holds his hands up as a smirk spreads across his face. "I know, I know ladies, I should have said only the best people, but all that P.R. B.S. aside, no set of tits has ever passed my class, sorry gals, but none of you strike me as having any more of a chance than the chicks before you. So, let's just…" Ryan notices a smirk on the face of the Latino female, and hot anger rises from his chest as he stops talking and rushes to stand in front of her, his face inches from her own.

"Excuse me Senorita but has something I've said in English translated into something laughable in Espanola?" He expects for her cockiness to melt, for her arrogance to shrivel, but it does not, instead, her eyes look straight into his own as if he is a small inconsequential thing to neither be feared nor respected.

"No, sir. I was just wondering if a broken nose would shut that racist, sexist mouth of yours…sir!"

Her matter of fact response takes him off balance and for a moment he feels unsure, insecure and afraid. Then he realizes that this is a woman and colleagues of his, other men, are watching her disrespect him. He knows he must put her in her place, he knows he must take charge and he knows he must regain the upper hand but it's what he doesn't know that makes his day so bad.

Had he bothered to read the profiles of this year's upper classmen, he would have learned that this "doable Mexican broad" is a medal of honor winning ex-marine and Krav Maga specialist. That her name is Dominica Verez and her recruiter underlined his short comments about her in her file: Tenacious and unrelenting!

Perhaps had Ryan known any of these things this day wouldn't have gone so badly for him. His chest swells, eyes grow wide, not with rage but in a feeble attempt at intimidating the small woman before him.

"I'll tell you what Mommasita, you break this nose and you'll be the first split tail to pass this class, so how about…" The last thing he remembers is seeing her forehead come forward followed by a crunching sound then blackness.

CHAPTER 2

Ware County, Georgia

An elderly man sits in a rocking chair on the porch of a home on stilts. Between his chair and another, a revolver sits atop a small table. The front door of his home appears to have been kicked in and, on the porch, near the top of the steps, lay several rifles, a jar of spare change and a tray with old collector's coins.

The old man rocks back in his chair as he lights a cigarette. Beside the revolver a large pitcher of iced lemonade sweats in the swamp heat and the old man looks down at the beverage as the sound of an approaching vehicle grows louder.

A small black truck emerges from beneath the low hanging branches of the willow tree beside the drive and all the sounds of the swamp bugs, birds and frogs go silent. A muffled noise is heard until the truck door opens and heavy rock music spills out into the sweltering heat of the day. The old man's face screws as he grimaces from the loud ruckus.

The driver, Richard Arwood Jr., looks up and realizes his uncle Ron Arwood is not pleased by the music and quickly reaches into the truck and turns the ignition off. "I didn't see you sitting there, Unc'!" Rich Jr. confesses as he shuts the door and makes his way toward the steps. The young man stops as he notices the pile of items on the porch and the damaged door.

"What the hell's going on Unc'?" Ron appears not to notice and exhales a cloud of cigarette smoke. "Never mind that! What in the hell took you so damn long?" The old man asks stubbing out his butt before lighting another; Rich Jr. examines the pile of rifles on the porch.

"I stopped off at the diner for breakfast...what's the emergency; first frost ain't for months yet?" "This ain't got nothing to do with no weed! I can't get cha to come around anymore lessen there's money in it for ya," Rich Jr. looks up, visibly ashamed, "Ah, hell Unc'! It ain't like that it's just..." "Shut the hell up and stop interruptin' me. That was a comma not a period!" Ron interrupts his nephew.

"Now as I was about to say, I hear tell yer tryin' to get a job as a turnkey in Ocilla up in Irwin County? This true?" Rich Jr. shrugs his shoulders. "What else am I gonna do? I'm eighteen and still livin' at my folk's house. I gotta work somewhere and bein' a C.O. is easy, no work and I can get the job even though my G.E.D. score was just enough to pass the test...They don't care how smart ya' are, they'll hire anybody. Only other job in these parts is melon farms. Picking melons is hard work."

Ron puts out his cigarette and looks at his nephew for a long moment. "Get ya' a glass of lemonade, you look hot boy."

Rich Jr. goes into the house as Ron lights another cigarette. The boy returns with two glasses and holds one out to Ron. Ron declines and Rich pours himself one before taking a long drink. Rich Jr. looks at the door again, "what happened to the front door, Unc'?"

Ron appears to not have heard the question. "You know I's in prison before, right?" Ron asks as Rich Jr. sits in the other chair "Well yeah, Unc', you told me...you said you went a couple of times back in the day." Ron takes a drag from his cigarette and sits back in his chair.

"Let me tell ya something I learned my first tour. Those with too much ambition might be prison inmates for a while, but those with no ambition will be prison guards for life! – I'm gonna tell you now, I'd rather see you dead than to see you bein' a worthless crap sack lockin' other humans up behind bars and concrete. I'd rather see you dead; at least you would have left this earth with dignity."

"But what else am I supposed to do? I have to work somewhere Unc'? "Not as no damn half-assed cop ya don't!" Ron exclaims. Rich Jr. appears to have thought of something, "You don't have to worry about me talking about what we do here, Unc', I wouldn't say nothin' to nobody."

Ron looks across the swamp and sees a young man on a fan boat. Rich Jr. looks up in time to see the guy on the fan boat wave at them before passing by. "Tom Haas? What's he doin' out here cookin' meth in a tent somewhere?" Ron raises an eyebrow. "You ever tried meth before?"

Rich Jr. spits off the porch, "Never, it's poison but I see everyone in town, everyone my age, running around with those little brown vials that Tom sells." Ron reaches into his pocket and produces a brown glass vial. Rich Jr.'s eyes grow big. "You do that crap, Unc?"

Ron smirks, "Hell no, you idiot! I want you to listen and listen to me carefully because you're too young to know it right now but if you get older it'll depend on how this visit goes today. I'm going to ask you a few questions and hope it goes the way we both want it to because you're just too stupid to understand what's happenin' here."

7

Rich Jr. looks around and shrugs, "what's the questions, Unc'?" Ron shakes his head and takes the revolver and places it in his own lap. Rich Jr. does not notice the gun.

"I'm seventy-two years old boy, got no family of my own 'cept you, yer' ma and pa, and both of them hate me. I've been smokin' these damn things since I's nine and I'm sure I got the cancer somewhere in my lungs, brain or ass...somewhere. Point is, I got some cash stashed, this land and house, my weed business, but most importantly, I got my dogs. You know I make the toughest damn dog on God's green earth, and when ya was younger you used to want one of 'em for yer own...you still want one?"

Rich Jr. sits up straight in his chair, "You mean one of your fighting dogs? You know I do Unc'; more than anything!" Ron's hand relaxes on the gun in his lap, "I'm gonna make you an offer and I hope for your sake, and mine, that you answer correctly...If I leave it all to you; the land, the house, the money, my weed business and my dogs...if I leave you my last grand champ as your first sire, show ya how to breed 'em and train 'em, if I leave ya everything, will you turn away from this shit idea of bein' a sorry screw?"

Rich Jr. appears to be thinking, and Ron's grip tightens on the pistol in his lap but relaxes when Rich Jr. responds, "I'd do whatever you want Unc', but what's a screw?" Ron ignores the question.

"It'll take a few years, but you move in with me, help out with everything, I'll pay ya, show ya all ya need to know and everything I got will be yours one day. The house, the land and all. My last champ will be yours, your very own monster."

Rich Jr. stands up with a smile on his face, "Hell, I'll go get my stuff now Unc'!" Ron shakes his head, "No ya won't, first things first. I need you to take them guns inside and put 'em back in my gun cabinet. Then we're gonna fix my door and besides you don't need to be drivin' until that shit gets out'a your system."

Rich Jr. appears confused, "What happened to your door Unc' and why's them guns out? Wait, what? What do you mean I don't need to drive 'til that shit's out of my system? What are you talking about Unc'?"

Ron points at the lemonade, "The meth, Tom said it'll take about a half hour to kick in and two days to wear off." Rich Jr. looks down at the pitcher in disbelief, "You put meth in the lemonade?"

Ron stubs out his cigarette, "To tell the truth...I's gonna kill ya." Rich Jr.'s eyes grow large, "What the hell are you talkin' about?" Ron stands up and stretches, "If you was still wantin' to be a turnkey before you left." Rich Jr. looks around, "What the hell did meth in the lemonade have to do with anything?"

Ron appears to be getting agitated, "For the story I's gonna have to tell the county pigs...that you came over all hopped up on drugs kicked in my door and went to stealin' my stuff, when they did the autopsy they'd find the dope in your blood and I'd walk free or close to it." Rich Jr. looks at the door and then the pile of rifles and coins. He turns pale as he realizes how well planned the old man's plot was and how he walked straight into it, how close he came.

"You don't think I'd have ever told on what we do, do ya, Unc'?" Ron lays the pistol down on the little table. "I never thought about it." Rich Jr. turns as his uncle walks past him, "Then why was ya gonna kill me?" "Ain't no kin of mine ever working' as a turnkey...like I said...I'd rather see you dead first," Ron responds as he enters the house. Rich Jr. shakes his h9ead in disbelief.

CHAPTER 3

The office is cold and small, the silence is nerve-racking but broken by the periodic turn of a page as the classification coordinator studies Verez's file. The woman is stern looking with salt and pepper hair, cut just below her ears. Her name is A. Wilkerson and as Verez reaches "Arlene" in her mental list of possible 'A' names, A. closes the file and looks up at Verez before pushing the folder away.

"The footage of your's and Ryan's incident was shown to Deputy Director Lawson. The audio as well as the video, and he agrees with Ryan's decision." A. says stoically. Verez begins to get a sickly feeling in her stomach, somewhere between how one feels being called to the principal's office and how one found guilty feels just before sentencing. "It must have been hard watching your father die like that, in front of you, at such an age? Then you went to live with your aunt in New York and when she died you joined the Marines at nineteen, what, to pay for college?" A. asks rhetorically before she continues,

"Then after two tours in Iraq, you came back to the states and decided, with no family left, why not join the Bureau, huh? I can't recall ever having approved any agent with such a tumultuous past. You've had a rough one kiddo." Verez feels it, understands the words between the lines. She knows she will not be an agent of the Federal Bureau of Investigations, but she cannot let go -- "tenacious and unrelenting."

"I do not bring baggage into my work," she says more as a departing remark rather than a statement of information. "Top of your law class at NYU, Medal of honor in Iraq, and now here...being the first woman to ever pass Ryan's testis class...no, I'd say you don't bring baggage, you've turned it into fuel."

Verez takes a deep breath, appears confused and is about to ask something. A. seems to have anticipated the question, "Ryan challenged you and he passed you as soon as he was released from the hospital. Lawson requested the video because he wanted to see a woman finally give Ryan what he's been asking for the past ten years. In fact, you're already assigned a post. Hearing about you passing the Ryan Course, Charles Casey in Atlanta requested for you down in the eleventh district.

Congratulations Verez, you're on your way to the empire state of the south. A.'s poker face fades and Verez is surprised to see it replaced by a motherly smile.

"When am I to report?" Verez asks anxiously. "Within seventy-two hours. Casey is very meticulous and I'm sure an apartment, vehicle, and office will already be waiting for you upon arrival...Hell, he may have you a wardrobe and boyfriend waiting, knowing Chuck."

A. and Verez look at one another as an uncomfortable silence comes between them. "Well, what are you waiting for? Seventy-two hours isn't long enough for you to sit around looking at me all day." A.'s motherly appearance fades.

Verez nods as she stands and starts for the door. "Verez," A. calls. Verez turns to see the smile. "Do us proud." A's face is warm once again. "I will represent the agency to the best of my ability," Verez responds. "I wasn't talking about the Bureau Verez, I was taking about us. Stay Strong." Verez nods and walks out into the hall.

Directly across from A's office, Verez walks into the bathroom. Her heart is beating fast as she stands facing the mirror above the sink. She stares, wide-eyed, ahead but gone is the mirror, and the reflection of herself has changed to that of a ten-year-old girl setting a table in a small but comfortable home.

The girl suddenly stops preparing the table and turns to look out of the window. A smile brightens her face before she dashes out of the front door. In the yard she finds her father, Raul Verez, getting out of his patrol
car. He smiles at his daughter but the smile fades as another car pulls up behind his own and four Hispanic men get out.

From the other side of the fence she watches, helplessly, as the men surround her father.

"Go back inside Dominica!" Her father demands just before the men attack him.

As she screams for them to stop, another man exits the other car. She cannot make out his features beneath the brim of the hat he wares.

With a signal from the faceless man the men stop kicking her downed father. "Your father should have taken me up on my offer...he forgot that he's not one of them, that he's one of us.

He forgot who he is. He forgot who I am, don't grow up to be like him." The shadow man says before putting a cigarette into his mouth and lighting it. The flames dance upon his features but still he cannot clearly be two streams of smoke from his nostrils extinguish the flame of the lighter. Dominica watches as he immediately produces a chrome revolver and, without hesitation, shoots her father four times in the chest as he lies on the ground.

The four men quickly get back into the car and before the fifth man casually climbs in, he turns to look back at the sobbing child a moment before he to gets in and the car speeds away.

Dominica opens the gate and drops to her knees placing her father's head on her lap.

"Daddy don't die! Please...I need you Daddy!" she pleads

Weak and coughing blood Raul looks up at his sobbing little girl..."Stay strong...Stay strong and you will never need anyone Dominica. Stay strong..." His last words fade with one last gasp before the crying child screams into the night.

"NO Daddy! Please!"

The sound of the door swinging open pulls Verez from the "memory's" clutches.

She's heard a military psychologist speak of flashbacks and the videos and pamphlets describe exactly what her "memories" feel like.

They began soon after she arrived in New York City to live with her father's sister, "Aunt Lupe", she would call her. "Aunt Lupe" was a very providing and responsible guardian. The small apartment stayed frigid and was even colder when Aunt Lupe was home from one of her two regular jobs.
An extreme catholic Robot and Aunt Lupe never once asked Dominica to talk about that night.

Soon the "memories" came like heat waves, She would feel as if the apartments forty five degrees would almost instantly rocket to a hundred and she felt as if the air in the apartment lost all its oxygen content and felt like a fish out of water.

The high school counselor described them as "panic or anxiety attacks". She was a nice little round Puerto Rican woman who was always in good spirits and eager to listen.

Unfortunately, this was five years after Dominica had first arrived.

Five years of Aunt Lupe caused any moments of familiarity to be painfully uncomfortable...

At first, she wanted to become a prosecutor and worked hard in high school and then it came time to reach out to colleges and a few extended their hands, but she needed a full scholarship.

She was very impressed with N.Y.U. and its School of Law. They had no objections with her enrolling, providing she secured the tuition. Even with the minority and government funds and her father's officer's family benefits she was over thirty thousand short and then, one day while passing a parking lot to get to the laundry-mat Dominica saw, in big bold words, **"College tuition benefits"**. She stepped in the small office of law and by spring break she was stationed in Israel, training in Urban Warfare and hand to hand combat.

Benjamin Nosson, the Krav-Maga expert and instructor of the Israeli special forces and the KIDON branch of Massad witnessed Dominica's training. Word spread that Nosson described the "Pretty Little American's Training." As "disturbingly violent" and "intense".

Her marine sergeant and drill instructor's comments, highlighted in her profile, stick out like neon lighting to those interested in single minded task mastering and machine-like precision. Coupled with a work ethic that seems rather extreme to even the most hard-nosed slave driving boss. It's enough to overlook the psychological atom bomb she survived as a child, when she witnessed the brutal murder of her father, and her obvious lack of human emotion skills.

Her "memories" are their "flashbacks." She knows, but she feels a searing stab of embarrassment for even acknowledging it or it's diagnosis and so talking about it with professionals is absolutely out of the question.

Verez splashes a bit of cold water onto her face at the sink before drying with a paper towel and exiting the bathroom.

CHAPTER 4

Rich Jr. is up and in the kitchen as Ron exits his room, the old man looks around the home before sitting at the table. "What the hell you doing up so early for? You ain't been up before me since you moved in." Rich Jr. brings a cup of coffee and sits in front of him. "Today's the day we breed Black and Valkyrie. I can't wait to get started. "It's been over a month and you said today was the day." Rich Jr. pleads excitedly.

"Today is the day, but you better listen to what I'm about to tell ya cuz you won't get but one chance to screw up around ol' Black and he'll kill ya for it." Ron warns examining the coffee.

"You tell me to stay clear of 'em and feed 'em through the fence, but he ain't growled at me once. Whenever I come around his nubby little tail wags away every time he sees me." Rich Jr. explains. Ron looks up at him. "He won't growl, doesn't want to scare ya off, and that nubby little tail will still be a waggin' while he's rippin' yer' fool throat out. He's a killer, nuttier than squirrel shit. I raised 'em from a pup and I can't get near 'em." Ron informs before taking a drink of the coffee and grimacing.

"What's wrong Unc', you don't like the coffee?" Rich Jr. asks disappointed. "I suppose chewin' the beans 'ed be worse." The old man pushes the cup away. "What happened to 'em Unc', you know, to make 'em so crazy?" Ron starts for the coffee before thinking better of it and taking a last drag from his cigarette.

"About thirty years ago I was in Brushy Mountain State Prison up in Tennessee. And in the movie room, they showed us one of them Geographic pictures. It was about Tasmanian devils, and how the male devil'll run in the den of the bitch devil. He'll chew'er up and breed'er all at once for a couple of days on end. Well them devils is so dam hopped up on rage and crazy that the female gets tired of being chewed on after the pregnancy takes. She turns on the male and runs 'em away. Them baby devils is so dam mean they's born fighting. I got to thinkin'...what if I could get my dogs crazy like that? Would my puppies be as aggressive? Well you know the answer to that?" Ron lights another cigarette.

"Well how do you get 'em crazy Unc', and how'd you get Black as crazy as he is?" Rich Jr. takes the cup and pours the motor oil looking substance into the drain.

"Easy...I take a cattle prod to 'em." Answers Ron, matter of fact like.

Rich Jr. turns in shock, "A cattle prod? Jesus Unc' can't that kill 'em? How many times do you hit 'em with it?" Ron exhales a cloud before answering his nephew. "I've only killed a half dozen or so...mostly been the bitches, but I don't have any number of time? Each dog's different, some go crazy after an hour or so and some take all day to turn."

Rich Jr. seems unable to believe what he is hearing and sits down at the table. All day? Jesus, that sounds terrible. How do you know...I mean how can you tell they have had enough?" He asks almost as if he doesn't really want to know.

"They get to talkin'...it's this whinin' growlin' noise and they all do it. May take a few hours, or all damn day, but sooner or later they all get to talkin'." Ron responds with pride.

"That's what happened to Black? Why don't he talk?"

Ron thinks about the question as he stares off into nowhere before a smile comes to his face.

"Black use to talk, couple years ago he up and stopped. See when they talk, they's crazy and senselessly violent...takes somethin' mighty strong to get 'em out of it. That's how I figured it anyway."

Rich Jr. appears not to be satisfied with the answer. "Yeah, but Black is crazy, you said, so why's he not still talking?"

Ron exhales another cloud before answering. "He's bat shit crazy alright, but the difference is he started likin' it. It's not most dog's nature to want to kill everything...it's a rare dog to be sure, and Black's one of a kind. He wants to kill the world." Ron smiles.

"Well, why don't you fight 'em anymore then, Unc'. I mean wouldn't he be perfect for fightin'?" Rich Jr. appears to be baffled.

Ron looks at him as if he said the stupidest thing possible. "He wants to kill the world stupid! Turn 'em loose on a dog in a pit around a crowd and he'll attack everything with a heartbeat.

Rich Jr. seems to understand, but then looks up and Ron knows another question is coming. "How the hell do we breed 'em then, Unc'?" Ron lights another cigarette and takes a long draw before exhaling.

"We strap Valkyrie over the layin' log. The one out back that's laid out near the barn. Then we muzzle'er and take the cattle prod to 'er till she starts takin'. Then I'm gonna lasso Black from outside his pen and thread the other end of the rope back through the chain linked fence...I want you to pull the other end tight, keep that son of a bitch pinned to the fence while I get the muzzle on 'em. I don't care if you choke the bastard out. Pull it tight cuz if he bites me. I'm gonna stomp a mud hole in yer' ass and walk it dry. Get it?"

Rich Jr. looks up, "Yeah, I hear ya, Unc'. I'll pull it hard...then what do we do?" Ron stubs out the cigarette. "Then we strap 'em over Valkyrie." Rich Jr. nods his head. "Then we're done huh?"

Ron shakes his head. "No, we ain't done. Black don't know how to screw, all he knows is kill."

Rich Jr. looks confused. "Then how the hell are we gonna get 'em to breed with her?"

Ron smiles. "You ever given a crazy pit bull a hand job before?"

Rich Jr. looks disgusted, "No!" Many hours later, as the sun is going down, Ron stands beside Rich Jr., who is on his knees, arms jerking between Valkyrie and Black with a look of pure disgust on his face.

Ron laughs loudly. "Black's done got 'em self-two cherries at once! Don't keep it all to yourself, we're tryin' to make puppies...when it swells up and gets to vibratin' slip it up in 'er!"

* * *

CHAPTER 5

Her office is small; just big enough for the desk, a chair on each side and one file cabinet. No window, she notices, and the chairs on either side of the desk are the same as the ones she saw in the break room when the secretary gave her the building tour. Verez begins to unpack when the door opens and she becomes trapped between it and the cabinet.

"Excuse me." Verez demands as the door closes allowing her to escape from the enclosure.

When the door opens once more a well built salt-and-peppered-hair man with grey eyes enters the small office. If she knew nothing more about the man, his stance and posture alone gives it away she thinks to herself.

"Director Casey, and I've reviewed your file, and what the Agency had on you was such an interesting read that I decided to make a few calls and catch up on your military history... The Al Hilah incident was a very traumatic experience according to your fellow marines? Casey says waiting for a show of surprise on the rookie's face.

The "Al Halah incident" was a special ops classified maneuver that was read by resistance black guardsmen as a coordinated attack. The marines were prepared for maneuvers and were taken off guard by an attack they expected as part of urban training.

Verez's Mossad training in urban warfare along with her tenacity and fearlessness showed through and her report of the incident was the only account that did not mention her heroics of the day.

But it's not surprise that Carey reads on his newest agents face, in fact her face tells him nothing.

"Retired two-star general Charles Casey, entered the Vietnam War with the Thirty Fifth Marine division in nineteen seventy-one. The "Than Hoa offensive" would have been the "Than Hoa debacle" if not for you blowing up the bridge." She doesn't expect him to show surprise but knows he has to be.

"I understand. I think you will be very good in the capacity of which I intend to use you." This time he registers a slight twitch of her left eyelid.... slight but still noticeable.

"Relax Agent, I intend to let you loose like a bullet, but do not forget a bullet moves in the direction it's aimed. Where "I" aim you. You report directly to me and me alone... Understand?" He says as cool as if he were a big box store manager.

"Yes, sir." Verez replies in a clip as if she were a marine once again.

"How long until you are settled in and prepared for your first assignment?" Casey asks.

"I'm settled and prepared now." She stands as if the assignment requires her immediate exit of the office.

"Relax Verez, I'll have the files brought to you. The investigation is now six months long. Our suspect Nash Vance is a real socialite, His real estate firm is the largest in the South East. If that's not bad enough, the guy eats lunch with the Mayor and donates boat loads of cash to build civic centers and hospital wings." Casey explains.

"Sounds like Mr. Wonderful.....What do we suspect him of doing?" Verez questions.

"Mr. Wonderful. I like it. Well, we calculate about thirty percent of the Atlanta's Narcotics trade is directed by Mr. Wonderful and three bodies and one missing person can be connected with him in some way shape or form and the deaths and disappearance of these people comes shortly after they attempted to witness or testify against him." Casey informs her.

"Well then, I guess I'll start studying up on... Nash Vance, is it? I'm ready when you are boss."

"You might take other cases and help in raids or investigations, but Nash Vance is Priority One... Get it!" Casey explains.

"Yes sir." Verez responds

"Anastasia was right about you I see." Casey turns to leave.

"Anastasia?" Verez asks.

"Yes, Anastasia Wilkerson... Your Quantico Coordinator." Casey responds.

"So, that's what the "A" stood for," Verez nods her head.

"Tell me about...always seemed more like an Arlene to me." Casey says before leaving the office. Verez shakes her head with a smile.

THE BRINDLE

* * *

CHAPTER 6

Pregnancy swells Valkyrie. She is strapped down, lying on her side, to a wooden plank. Her head is encased in a large metal box with tennis ball sized holes so she can breathe and be fed. A constant whining noise echoes from within the metal box as Ron and Rich Jr. look at her from the other side of her pen.

"She's ready to pop, be late night or early mornin' but she's ready." Ron explains while exhaling a cloud.

Rich Jr. looks at the miserable creature. "Does she have to be strapped down like that long after she's had 'em?" he asks with a note of pity in his voice.

"She'll kill 'em otherwise...the bitch is crazy. She ain't got a mother's instinct now. We keep 'er restrained 'til they're old enough to start natural selection." Ron flips the cigarette.

"Then we'll let her loose of that board and box?" Rich Jr. hopes.

"Yeah, if she has a litter of only males we will. If she has any little bitches...well, then we won't need her no more once the bitch pup's old enough to eat solid food." Ron explains.

"Then what do we do with her if she does have any females?" Rich Jr. asks hoping it's not what he thinks.

"Feed'er to the gators. What use is a crazy bitch? More trouble than she's worth. Already got one psycho dog on my hands...don't need another to have to worry about!"

Rich Jr. listens to the whining coming from the box and decides it might be better for the poor creature if she does have female pups.

"Well, come get me as soon as she has 'em." Ron orders as he turns to go back to the house.

"I'll have to stay out here all damn night? What if we..."

"As soon as she shits 'em out put 'em to her teets and then come and wake me up?" Ron demands halfway to the house.

Rich Jr. looks back at the bloated whining dog and begins to feel sorry for her as well.

It's nearly sun up before she has the last of them. Rich Jr. does as he is told. "She's had 'em Unc'! She's had five of 'em!" He exclaims as he enters Ron's room.

The old man leaps out of bed. "Alright! Calm the hell down!" Ron yells as he starts putting his boots on and has a coughing fit before lighting a cigarette. "Any black one like ol' Black?" Ron asks as he ties the laces of one boot.

"Yeah, two of 'em. Both are males. There's a brown female like Valkyrie too and a gray, smoke colored male," Rich Jr. explains.

Ron waits a moment before looking up at his nephew. "I thought you said there was five of 'em...that's four stupid!" Ron bends to tie his boot.

"Yeah, a male...he's all sorts of colors; brown, black, white and..."

"Son of a bitch!" Ron growls as he jumps up and storms past Rich Jr.

"What the hell's wrong, Unc'?" Rich Jr, asks as he follows Ron out into the backyard.

In Valkyrie's pen Ron uses his Zippo lighter to check the color of the last male pup. Rich Jr. watches from the open gate. The lighter flips shut as Ron stands, "It's a god dammed Brindle!" He exclaims as he pushes past Rich Jr. to go back into the house. Rich Jr. follows.

"What the hell's the matter? The color...the Brindle color? What's wrong with his color?" Rich Jr. asks all the way into the house. Ron ignores the boy as he sits in the kitchen table and lights a cigarette.

Taking a seat across from Ron, Rich Jr. continues his questioning, "What's the big deal? It's just a dog's coat color. Why are you so upset?" The boy wonders. Ron's eyes fall onto his nephew as if seeing him for the first time and hearing him only just then.

"In my line, the Brindles are worthless for fighting. They ain't no good for nothing!" Ron says before taking a long drag of his cigarette.

"How's the color of its hair change anything? It just don't make sense." Rich Jr. says shaking his head. Ron stubs his cigarette out in the overflowing ashtray.

"Listen stupid! I know my line. You think hair don't make a difference? That may be true for other lines but mine has been this way for nearly fifty years now. They don't change. I thought I'd bread the bastards out completely. It's a good thing it's a male and not our only female or we'd have to keep Valkyrie's crazy ass around." Ron explains before lighting another cigarette. Rich Jr. shakes his head and Ron elaborates.

"The damn thing is not good for fightin'. They're smart as whips, every Brindle in my line is, but they ain't cut out for hard livin' and don't have the killer instinct. It's been this way ever since I screwed up fifty years ago and introduced one into my line. Me and your pa', he was just a boy then, had gotten dogs from Uncle Ray. He's been dead for thirty years now. You never knew Ray. Well they was both pups but two different litters. Your pa' kept his for a pet and I made mine a moneymaker. Named 'em Duke and boy was that bastard somethin'? By his prime he was pullin' ten cinder blocks and whoopin' everything that was put in front of 'em." Ron seems to fade into the past, as he speaks his eyes wander toward the ceiling.

"Yeah ol' Duke was somethin' alright. He stared gettin' old though and his hips started to give like most pit bull's hips do, so I decided to look for a female to breed 'em with, but like a fool I was greedy and put 'em in one last fight. Serves me right, he won, but somehow or 'nother the other dog got his balls and just chewed 'em up so good there was no breedin' him. I panicked and went to Uncle Ray, he was fresh out of males in Duke's line but Duke's sister was there. I didn't have a male worth breeding anywhere in the county. So, I borrowed your pa's dog. He was a Brindle and when the pups come out they were worthless, everyone! Smart as nails, but brains isn't what a fightin' dog needs. They need to be ruthless and have that killer instinct. Lucky for me I violated my parole and went back to prison before anyone found out my dogs were all pussies. While I was in I got the idea to breed the Brindles out of my line and came up with the natural selection trick. At first, I'd have two in this litter and three in the next, but slowly they started fallin' off and I'd get two generations or so without having any of 'em and the last four of my litters haven't had a one in 'em, so I thought for sure they was gone. But, here the little Brindle bastard is!" Ron lights another cigarette.

Rich Jr. thinks on what he's heard the looks up, "What if..."

"You get dumber by the day don't ya' boy? Did you not hear what I said? They ain't cut out for hard living! They's all weak! I ain't had a Brindle make it to second, let alone be the last one left! They're smart, real smart, but brains ain't important! They need to be vicious and Brindles ain't vicious in my line!" Ron explains.

Rich Jr. sits up and puts his hands on the table. "I hear what you are sayin; Unc', I do, but what if you had a Brindle make it through the natural selection? Wouldn't a smart bad ass dog be somethin'? Think about it for a..."

"You just don't get it! Alright, alright hard head I'll show ya'. Usually I put the little bastard out of their misery before the mother's milk gets wasted on 'em but to show you this little shit will have to suffer. You'll see for yourself, that way when I'm gone you won't waste time on 'em either," Ron concludes.

Rich Jr. sits back content to have won an argument with his uncle for once. Rich Jr. feels it, knew it before he ever told the old man about the puppy with the coat of many colors. There's something about it. Something he cannot explain. Learning what its history is in Ron's line makes him root for the little underdog that much more.

The puppy is not the only special life brought into the world this night. Rich Jr. has no way of knowing, but over two thousand miles away, another life is beginning. Without one another neither will seem very remarkable. Together, however, they will work a miracle. But for now, fate must be left to figure out how to go about bringing them together.

CHAPTER 7

Orange County, California

The door opens slowly as a sliver of light from the hallway illuminates the dark room just enough for a man to get his body through the door. He shuts it silently before he makes his way to the bed of an attractive woman resting with a bundled blanket on her chest. He bends down and kisses her forehead. Her eyes flutter open.

His name is Jacob Hertzle and she is Sarah Hertzle, his wife, the bundle in her arms is Jasmine Hertzle, four hours old. "I told the nurse at the desk that I would only be a few minutes. I just want to see the two of you once more before I go home," he whispers.

"I wish we could go home with you," Sarah says hoarsely,

Sarah follows Jacob's eyes to the bundle on her chest before she pulls a fold of the blanket back revealing the newborn whose eyes are open and looking blindly up at the ceiling.

"She's so quiet...she's not cried once since she was born. She's such a good little angel!" Sarah dotes.

"She's beautiful, just like her mother." Jacob can't take his eyes from the child.

"She's so calm and quiet, she's an introvert, like her father...a deep thinker," Sarah jokes.

I'll have to get going, but I'll be back first thing in the morning to take both of my little ladies back home." He promises. Jacob kisses the child's head and his wife's lips.

"I wish we could go home with you honey. Be here early," She play pouts.

"Dr. Levine said they will run a few routine tests in the morning, but once they've finished, you will both be released," he reminds her.

"I still want you here early. You know how hospitals creep me out." Sarah pleads.

"I will be, I'll beat the morning smog over West Hills. I promise." One kiss to each of his ladies and Jacob quietly exits the hospital room.

Sarah watches him depart before turning her attention to her daughter. "You are going to be such a spoiled rotten little girl. Yes, you are. Your daddy is going to spoil you rotten, little lady." Sarah gently brushes her finger against the warm, soft cheek of the baby's face.

For a moment Sarah can do nothing but beam with pride as she stares at the beautiful face of the child in her arms, but an overwhelming feeling comes over the new mother. She cannot explain it, but she feels that something is not as it should be and the smile dissolves slowly into a look of concern.

CHAPTER 8

Casey closes his office door and looks across the darkness of the unoccupied cubicles and empty offices, to the one lone light radiating from beneath a closed door. He walks towards the light. With a knock and acknowledgment from within, Casey opens the door to find Verez pouring over stacks of paperwork.

Pictures of Nash Vance, from surveillance teams, adorn the walls and a pyramid of possible soldiers and underlings support the capstone with Vance's debonair profile at the pinnacle. Casey leans against the open door.

"Talking about being his biggest fan, if you weren't investigating the guy I'd swear you were the most meticulous stalker I've ever seen."

Verez looks up and around her little cover, "Oh, yeah, huh? I started with a few pictures and the next thing you know I'm an avid collector of all things Nash Vance."

"Well Verez, in the last three months or so we've accumulated more material evidence on Vance and his operation than we had in the entire six months of our investigation prior to your arrival. You've also managed to net us another key witness, which was magic in and of itself. You're the first person in, and the last out, each and every night. Don't think I have not noticed," he comments.

"What's Larry's story anyway, disgruntled employee, turned over a new leaf, found God...what?" Casey asks.

"He says he's wanting to make things right...you know, feeling guilty sort of story. I have a hunch he's been dipping into the honey jar and may have gotten caught sticky handed." Verez shrugs.

"What kind of dirt does he say he has on Vance? Has he shown you that he's even credible? I mean to nail Vance; a judge is going to want an air tight case. Hell, the Prosecutor's office wants a smoking gun in the Holy Grail just to ask for a warrant.

Larry better have something serious." Casey inquires.

"Well, he can put us in contact with a key witness Larry said, he's over the booking; that he makes sure the money, dirty or not, comes out of the other end clean and accounted for. He can do us two goods. The first, show us how Vance cleans the dirty money by taking yearly trips to Tunica, Mississippi, and Reno, Nevada. Second, he says the guy hates Vance, but likes breathing, so he works with him." Verez raises her eyebrows.

"Reno and Tunica, there's only one thing in Tunica, and since Reno has the same attractions, I guess it's safe to say Vance is using the casinos to clean his cash. That means it's basically a dead end for us on the money thing." Casey informs. Verez furrows her eyebrows."Why's that? I have some interesting numbers I obtained from Vance's financial statements." Verez digs around for a folder containing the papers.

"Don't bother, I know what you found. Let me guess, Vance has brought back a couple a million from each trip? It is wired by electronic cashier checks to his bank account each time his casino trip is over?" Casey guesses. Verez stops searching for the folder.

"Yeah, how did you know that?" She sits back and waits for the explanation.

"It's an old money laundering trick used by the big timers...The guy goes, bags full of cash, and spends a week at the casino. He purchases fifty grand in chips goes out on the floor for a little while, goes back to his room, drops the chips off, and goes down and gets fifty grand more, repeat, rinse and wash all day, every day, for a week straight. By the time his "vacation" is over, he has two or three million in chips. Takes them to the cashier and says "I can't believe my luck...can I have this wired to my account in B.F.E., or wherever, I don't want to have this kind of cash on me when I go back home. From there it's wired and considered earnings or winnings. He has to pay taxes, but if he's ever arrested, and we try to confiscate all that cash, we will have to take on his lawyers and the I.R.S." Casey explains.

"That's crazy? Why has nobody tried to get this stopped? The I.R.S., aren't they on our side?" Verez asks.

"There's too much money in it for everyone concerned...so no it's not going to be stopped anytime soon. The I.R.S. is on whose ever side pays the most taxes...we are tax exempt while he's paying for their protection." Casey explains. Verez just shakes her head.

"That's the bad news, however. The good news is, Larry can get us hooked up with this other fellow. Then we could learn the time and location of these drug and money swaps and flat out nail Vance's ass to the wall." Verez raises her eyebrows.

"So, concentrate on Larry's mystery man and let go of the casino stuff?" she asks.

"Yes, get Larry to put something in writing, heaven forbid he ends up like Randal, get this name as quick as possible out of him. I'll see you in the morning and...."

Casey's phone rings and he reaches into his jacket. Casey here."

Verez watches as Casey's face goes blank. She can tell the phone call is not a good one.

"Do you have a positive ID?" He asks the caller. It's a body, Verez guesses, or a suspect. Casey looks at her and it's when he shakes his head apologetically that she solves the riddle. Larry is dead.

A card was found in his wallet with the FBI office number on it. The county police wanted to know is he was one of theirs; an informant. Casey said that he was not, probably Verez concluded, to protect the investigation or perhaps because they had not gotten anything tangible out of him. Back to the drawing board. Game...Vance.

THE BRINDLE

***

CHAPTER 9

He's awoken by a high-pitched noise that calls to him. Something about the sound has kept him away from the hard box for months, but for reasons he will never know, tonight he must go to it. He slowly makes his way around the corner and peeks into the opening from where the sound emits.

He looks back to see if any of his siblings are awake, for he would feel much braver if they were with him. They all sleep in a knot together and he peers into the dark opening of the box, and the noise suddenly stops.

The smell is strong, but despite his instinct to get as far from the opening as possible, there is something in the scent that urges him forward. Sniffing as he moves deeper into the opening, he finds a moment of resistance before one good push allows for his entire head to be within the box.

The smell is powerful within, but his eyes adjust to the darkness, the sound comes, loud, so loud it rattles his eyes as they adjust fully and there, only inches from his snout, are the largest sharpest teeth he has ever seen. A feeling grips him, and though he does not know what it is, he is right to feel it because at this moment he should be terrified.

He cries out and pulls back as hard as the little muscles in his body will allow, but it is of no use, the more he pulls, the more he cries out. The whining growling insanity of his mother sputters, pauses, and as his sharp cries echo within the box, her talking stops.

Whether it is the sounds and smell of her child or the raw natural power of the mother's instincts, nobody may ever know. Whatever it is, Valkyrie, snaps out of it and the ranting of an insane creature becomes the lapping tongue kisses of a mother, who herself is trapped within the box. His panicked pulls become pushes as he attempts to get as close to her as the metal opening will allow.

He will spend this night in the company of love, and it is this one night which will instill within him a heart of gold which will withstand the wickedness of both time and man.

THE BRINDLE

CHAPTER 10

Rich Jr. runs into the house nearly causing Ron to spill his coffee as he sits at the table beneath his usual cloud of smoke. "She's killed one of 'em, Unc'! She's chewed his little head right off!" Rich Jr. accuses. "What the hell are you talking about, Fool?" Ron stands up and follows his nephew outside, across the backyard to the pen where Valkyrie and the puppies are.

Ron enters the pen, slapping the other puppies away. He gets down on his hands and knees and peers into the metal box that contains both Valkyrie and the Brindle's head. Instantly, Valkyrie begins growling and Ron can see the puppy is perfectly fine.

He realizes that Valkyrie's talking has stopped as she growls to protect her puppy. Looking into the metal box he sees that she is no longer crazy. "Welcome back bitch." Ron snarls as he pulls away from the box. "How old you say these pups are?" Ron asks his nephew as he gets back to his feet.

"Almost three months? Maybe a few days older? Why?" Rich Jr. asks, looking into the box.

"He's fine. Both of 'em are in there, lookin' back up at me. Reason is because they are old enough for natural selection. Take the female pup to the front pen and get her food and water. Take the three male pups to the back pen and don't give 'em shit. Take these two and put bullets in their heads and feed 'em to the gators. I know what yer' gonna say but it's his own damn fault for stickin' his head in there. I ain't cuttin' open my box just so that worthless bastard can live a few more days!" Ron demands.

"I can get his head out!" Rich Jr. drops down and begins pulling the Brindle's body.

The puppy cries out and Valkyrie begins growling and struggling to free herself. Just when Ron starts to tell his nephew stop, Rich Jr. frees the puppy.

He turns the animal loose and starts to stand when the Brindle dashes back to the box and stuffs his head back inside.

"Goddamn it!" Rich Jr. growls as he begins the rescue again. Ron watches in disgust as his nephew frees the protesting puppy once more and stands with the dog in his arms.

"I tell you what, Mother Teresa, you can take that little Brindle bastard back there with the rest of 'em but if that bitch ain't dead and fed to the gators by the time I'm done feedin' the sheriff, you can pack your shit and get the hell out! This ain't the business of no bleedin' hearts!" Ron snarls.

"Feedin' the sheriff? What the hell are you talking' about, Unc?" Rich Jr. asks.

"Takin' a shit stupid! Get it done!" Ron turns back to the house.

"Why kill 'er though? She ain't crazy no more," Rich Jr. pleads.

"We got a fresh female that's why! Now do it or get the hell out!" Ron says over his shoulder as he walks off.

As soon as the Brindle and his three brothers are locked into the pen, at the back of the property, he begins whining and jumping up on the fence looking into the direction where last he left his mother. The other males are busy sniffing and exploring their new territory, but he is concerned with one thing only and long after the sound of gunfire is heard, he continues to look in the direction he believes his mother to be.

Rich Jr. enters the house, exhausted and disgusted and flops into the chair across from his uncle, "I took care of everything. The female pup is watered and fed, Valkyrie's gone and the male pups are in the back pen. How long until we feed and water them?" Rich Jr. wonders.

"We don't." Ron replies before lighting a cigarette.

"What do you mean? They have to have food and water...they'll die?" Rich Jr. shakes his head.

"That's the whole point dummy!" His uncle blows smoke rings.

"I don't' get it? Why the hell..."

"Because," Ron interrupts, "the strongest puppy will live longest. The one that's healthiest after the others have died, or near it, will be the last one, they don't all have to be dead, just near it. Strength and willpower will keep a starving dog alive. Those without it will just curl up and accept their fate. That's not the kind of dog that becomes a grand champ!"

"Yeah, but Unc', no food, no water, don't you think that's a little harsh?" his nephew reasons.

"No! No, I don't! No food! No water! No pity! No kindness! No love! That's how you ensure; no fear, no mercy, no compassion and no losses! We're making a monster. Where another dog ends that's just where he'll begin! A ruthless killer trained every day to be a machine, incapable of losing or feeling fear. Make him hate life and he'll love to take it from other animals. Every day he will feel the pain of the training, chained to bricks and every step of his life will be a struggle until all he knows is the cold feel of steel links around his neck and the feel of aching muscles, pure misery. The only break he'll get is when his collar is broken so he can kill and he'll grow to enjoy the fighting more than breathing. He'll be a monster. He'll be a fighting dog's nightmare and they'll come from all over the country to put theirs against ours. They'll bring giants. They'll bring beast that you'd swear were unbeatable, but their animal can't win because of one very important thing. They lack the pure hatred of life, theirs as much as the others. Ours will hate life! His own especially and it's only when he does that that he becomes unbeatable. That's my secret. That's why my dogs never lose "

Rich Jr. sits back in his chair and tries to imagine such a life as miserable as the one his uncle describes. He cannot and so he stands up. "I got to take a shower. Kristine is expecting me to take her out tonight. She could be the one!" He says walking towards his bedroom. "Why ain't you ever had a good woman Unc'?" he asks from his room.

"Because they don't exist. I've had many I'd poke on for a couple a days or so but none I wanted around too long," Ron explains.

Rich Jr. stops on his way to take a shower, "That's a hell of a way to think, Unc'!" He starts to walk off.

"You'll learn after you go through a few of 'em. They're all evil." Ron claims.

"Not all of 'em, Unc'," his nephew corrects.

"I tell ya' they are, every last one of 'em. Any damn thing that bleeds every damn day for a week straight and don't die has gotta be evil!" Ron stabs a finger at his nephew for emphasis. Rich Jr. howls with laughter as he walks into the bathroom. Ron shakes his head.

* * *

CHAPTER 11

The night finds him still whimpering and standing facing the direction he knows his mother is in. The others, his brothers, sleep curled up together in the far corner of the pen. He will not risk sleeping for fear of missing even the slightest glimpse of her.

He had never felt the way he did that night he spent alone with her, and he will never forget that feeling as long as he lives. The pain in his stomach is strong, but contends with the pain of missing the sight of her and so far, the pain in his chest has won out over that of his belly.

The hours go by, the moon rises higher, and he is cold and alone, hungry and broken hearted. There is a movement in the grass to his left. He wants to look for her and whines in indecision as the movement grows closer until he chances one look and discovers a large black beetle.

Instinctively he bites down on the bug, only to find its prickly legs irritating his tongue. He shakes his head with his mouth open and slings the creature. The black beetle is injured and moves slower in an attempt to escape. The Brindle bites down on the bug again, and again is repelled, but now the beetle barely moves. One last bite and the puppy is free to enjoy his meal.

He discovers the bug has helped with the pain that is in his stomach, so he hunts through the grass for more creatures. The gray puppy awakens and sees his brother hunting, and so follows suit. Though the Brindle discovers the solution for the pain in his belly, it will be years before he finds a cure for the pain in his chest. Many years and many miles away.

Six days later Rich Jr. and Ron are standing outside the puppy pen looking down at the males. "Now how the hell is it possible that the two black ones are dead and these two are fresh as spring chicks?" Rich Jr. wonders.

"They've been eating on bugs and such and look at 'em lickin' the grass." Ron points at the gray and Brindle pups as they lick on the grass.

"What the hell are they licking grass for?" he asks.

"It's morning, they're getting the dew off the blades," Ron explains and Rich Jr. shakes his head in amazement.

"I'd say that Brindle probably figured it out and Smoke was smart enough to follow suit." Ron decides.

"Well, what do we do now, Unc', Keep 'em both?" his nephew hopes.

"Hell no! Your Brindle got this far, I'll give ya' that, but here's where the road ends! I told you they's smart and he's proven it but I also told ya' they's no good for fightin' and here's where I'll prove it."

Ron reaches into his overalls and pulls out a pocket knife and a hunk of beef jerky. He cuts two pieces and gives one to Rich Jr. "Give this to that Brindle bastard." He bends down and feeds Smoke a larger chunk. Rich Jr. feeds the exited Brindle pup.

Both pieces of meat are devoured in a fraction of a second before both puppies clamor and beg for another helping. Ron cuts another piece and looks at his nephew. "Got my money on smoke." He predicts before tossing the jerky between the animals.

The fact that they are brothers and have played and slept together all their young lives is not considered. For this moment is a matter of survival and in this moment the instincts locked within their DNA surface. Twenty generations of warriors' flow through their young veins and are unleashed upon one another in a flash of needle sharp teeth.

The Brindle bites down on the floppy ear of the brother and rage is release in the gray pup as he attempts to inflict the same wound on the Brindle. In his anger, the gray pup ignores his instincts to stay low and makes a fatal mistake as he rises to try and get on top of his brother. The Brindle spins on smoke and takes the gray pup off balance. Smoke tumbles over and the Brindle seizes the opportunity and attempts to get the throat of his downed opponent.

Smoke successfully pushes his fierce brother up and away from his throat, but the Brindle has gravity on his side and soon smoke is exhausted by the effort of pushing his brother's weight up.

The Brindle gets through his brother's defense and his instincts collide with his inexperience as he latches on to the gray puppy's neck, harmlessly biting down on the loose skin and shaking his head vigorously, though Smoke is not hurt, he is exhausted and has lost.

The Brindle, as if knowing he has beaten the odds, looks directly up into the angry eyes of Ron Arwood, Ron enters the pen and picks both puppies up, as he walks past Black's pen, he tosses the gray pup over the fence to Black who catches his son in midair. Ron does not bother to look as he continues to the middle of his yard with the Brindle.

And the victor wins a small chain collar around his neck; the collar is connected to a chain which is connected to a large red brick. The Brindle notices two tiny glass bowls. In one there is water in the other is ground beef.

He runs toward the bowls but a few feet from reaching them, he is yanked back. He gets up and tries for them again and is again stopped. He struggles, back paws digging into the ground until finally, the brick begins to slide. Inch by inch he struggles and inch by inch he moves closer until he finally reaches the food and water, which he devours instantly before noticing two more bowls further away.

Again, he struggles and again the brick begins to move. There are several portions each further than the next, and before the sun sets, he will have reached them all only to have to do it again the following day.

His victory, worse than pyrrhic, may be one he'd have been better off not winning for in this win he will be rewarded with suffering, the likes of which exist no scales to tally.

The days will be swamp hot and the nights spent in physical agony of the day's rigorous abuse of which those that abuse dogs call "training." To compact his torture, her memory, what might be thought of as sweet, will become searing for the realization will set in that she is gone and the feeling she brought will never be again.

As painful as those memories are he will cling to them until she no longer has a scent, a sound or an image. She will become a dream, a notion that will be swallowed in this nightmare he calls life but hold on to this painful notion he must. Like one clinging to a scorching hot ember in an arctic blizzard, for it is all he has.

The sight of Ron Arwood, the keeper of hell, will come to represent the dawn of misery as each sunrise will be followed by the chain smoking devil and his daily regimen of commands, kicks, and growls.

When he slips, makes the slightest mistake, he will be met with the toe of a boot, the edge of a board or the strike of a stick. Accomplishments mean only that he isn't struck and in that he finds his reward and knowing no other life, this is how his days, weeks, months and years shall be, and so, the "training of the Brindle has begun."

* * *

CHAPTER 12

Jacob and Sarah sit in the office of the pediatrician. In Sarah's arms, Jasmine Marie sucks on her fist quietly. The doctor enters and gives a sympathetic smile as he sits.

"Mr. and Mrs. Hertzle, the test results have been examined by both myself and Dr. Owens in Seattle, and I'm afraid that we've both found them conclusive...Jasmine is Autistic. Frankly, I am very surprised that you suspected it so early Mrs. Hertzle. We had to wait until now to run the tests, but we suspected months ago. Before we can diagnose the disorder, the child must be at least six months of age," the doctor explains.

Jacob sits up and leans on the desk. "So, what do we do? What can we do?" he asks.

Dr. Albert's eyes betray his pity for the parents. "The only thing to do Jacob is to love her and be patient. She's a child, depending on her level of functionality, she may need intensive attention for the rest of her life," Dr. Albert attempts to be honest and at the same time gentle.

"When you say functionality, what exactly are you talking about?" Sarah asks, not taking her eyes from the child in her arms.

"Individuals with Autism vary in their level of functionality. In some cases, they are very high functioning, most of those are Asperger's Syndrome. These people live very normal lives and even go on to have families of their own. On the opposite end of the Spectrum, you have low functioning Autistics and these individuals require a great deal of assistance their entire lives," Dr. Albert explains.

Jacob looks at the child in his wife's arms, "What brought this on? Neither of us drinks nor uses drugs. We're not related to one another...I mean how the hell did this happen?"

The doctor struggles to hold back a laugh, "It's not like that. Autism isn't a result of inbreeding or substance abuse, some people claim it's a result of childhood vaccinations, but it's not. It's as unpredictable as allergies, epilepsy or any other defect or disorder." He informs the couple.

"Why us? Why did this happen to us?" Jacob pleads.

The doctor grows impatient. "Let me tell you that I've seen parents whose children were born with congenital heart defects that gave them only enough time to hold their child once before it passes. This is your daughter and she's here and will live a long, and depending on you, happy life." The doctor mellows and Jacob sits back in the chair. "I have information here." He slides a file to Jacob, and Sarah leans over and grabs it. "There are support groups, websites, books and programs that can help you deal with the issues that may come with raising an Autistic child. As I said, each case is unique," he points out.

"Do you know what level Jasmine is at? I mean how high functioning she will be?" Sarah asks.

"At this stage, she is only six months old so there is no definite way of knowing. But if I had to say, I'd say fairly low. She will more than likely be detached, isolated and more often than not, she'll be in a world of her own and it will more than likely be that way for the rest of her life." As he speaks, tears well up in Sarah's eyes and the doctor hands her a box of tissues.

"So, what can we do?" the mother asks.

Dr. Albert pauses a moment before responding with the only answer he knows to give. "There is only one thing for you to do. Love her, guide her, give her plenty of attention and be patient with her. In short, be her parents, because that's what she needs most from you both."

Sarah looks down at the precious child in her arms and for a moment their eyes lock. Sarah swears to herself that she will be all the things her daughter needs in life; patient, loving and attentive. If she can be reached, Sarah vows to do whatever it takes to do just that. No matter what it takes.

CHAPTER 13

He tries to rise, but only manages to slide forward through the grass. He is larger, nearly a year old and dragging three cinder blocks on a chain, from his neck, day and night.

There are only two reasons the chains are removed. The first is to strengthen his bite force and neck muscles by being made to jump up and grip a knot in a rope that dangles from a tree branch. The second is to learn to balance on his hind legs. Each are daylong exercises that come once a week.

His longest hang time thus far from the rope is only seventeen minutes. He has still yet to rise to his back legs and this has angered Ron to no end, but today is the day. He has only moved forward through the grass like a sled propelled by his hind legs. His front legs have been secured to his chest by a vest fashioned for this very thing. The discomfort he has long gotten used to, but today he will learn to rise the hard way.

Ron and Rich Jr. walk toward the bound dog. Ron carries a chain and his nephew a burlap sack. Instinctively the Brindle slides toward them, mistaking their arrival to mean the time has come to be unbound as it has every other time for the last three months since this exercise began. However, this time, he won't be released from his torment, but rather taken to another level of hell beyond what he has ever known.

Ron secures the chain to the dog's neck and wraps the other end to the pole beside the barn. Rich Jr. then dumps what looks like dirt all around the bound animal before quickly moving away and slinging the bag aside. Ron opens the door of the barn wide, so that it is like a 'V', with the dog facing the corner where the hinges are. The dog is trapped between the barn wall and the open door.

Suddenly the dirt begins burning his lips, nose, ears, and eyelids as he yelps in pain. The dirt is alive, as Georgia fire ants angrily attack the helpless dog. The Brindle yelps and thrashes in anguish. His body whips side to side, slamming into the wall of the barn and the door which is being braced by Rich Jr.

The dog tries to back up but finds Ron's boot each time. The pain is excruciating, but suddenly, as he attempts to wipe the ants off by using the ground, he bends at the abdomen and nearly rises by mistake and crashes to the ground to be attacked more viciously. Again, he bends at the abdomen and rises. Ron splashes cold water over the dog's head which both soothes his pain and washes the angry red ants off.

The vertical escape is short lived as he collapses back to the earth to be attacked once more. Again, he rises, and again his anguish is washed away. The pattern teaches him and by the third day of hind leg balance training, the ants are no longer required but still he cannot stand long.

The year will become another and this second year will find him hanging from the rope knot for nearly two hours. He will also learn to stand on his hind legs for minutes at a time and begin pulling cinder blocks.

The third year will end being able to hang from the rope for five hours, hop on his hind, front legs bound like a kangaroo all around the yard and will pull nine cinder blocks day in and day out.

By the end of the fourth year, he can dangle from the rope knot eight hours at a time. He moves, still like a kangaroo, but gracefully in long leaps, with front legs bound, and may go over an hour without falling. His regular chain must be replaced with a forty-pound log chain as he drags twelve, seventeen-pound blocks, behind him day and night.

He also has three fights this fourth year and none of them last long enough for anyone of the men watching to wonder who the victor might be. The night after the last fight, Rich Jr. and Ron watch as the dog drags his twelve-block burden and chain around his massive concrete floor pen.

"He's something ain't he, Unc'? I'd hate to see him and ol' Black go at it...who'd you put your money on?"

Ron spits off the back porch before shaking his head. "Nope, wouldn't even be close. He'd kill ol' Black. In his prime Black was only pullin' ten blocks on a regular chain. We'll be hookin' up another block to him before too long. Don't get me wrong! Black's still more than another dog could take, but I ain't ever seen nothing like that damn Brindle. I've been harder on the son of a bitch than I ever was to any animal or woman my whole life and he's just gotten tougher for it. He's the smartest damn thing I ever saw to boot...when he looks at the other dogs, when he watches them, you can tell he's thinkin'. The son of a bitch is studyin' 'em. I just wish we could make him a killer. If we could make him hate, we could show 'em all the baddest damn dog to step in a pen." Ron declares looking at the animal.

Rich Jr. looks at his uncle as if he's crazy. "He's killed two of the three dogs' he's fought...I'd call him a killer." He tells Ron.

Ron shakes his head. "A killer wouldn't have let that second dog turn away...a killer would have went for the throat of that coward," Ron explains before lighting a cigarette.

"He seen the dog was done and let 'em be...he won the fight." But Ron is not listening.

"If he doesn't learn to hate we won't ever see him at his best. We have to get 'em to hate' Get 'em to hate, and I might take 'em to Alaska to fight grizzlies."

* * *

CHAPTER 14

East L.A., California

An exhausted and injured pit-bull lays on its side, unable to rise. Two Hispanic men stare down at it where it lays on the concrete floor of a large pit three feet below the surface they stand upon.

"We've fought him too much Diablo. Twice in two days is too much for any dog It's..."

"He's lost four of his last five fights! I'm done losing our money because of this bum ass mutt!" The long-haired Diablo declares before walking back to a work bench and grabbing a roll of duct tape.

"He's retiring." Diablo says as he drops into the pit and tapes the hind legs of the dog. Just above the paws, before doing the same to its front legs. Once finished, he tosses the tape to the side and pulls the dog out of the pit before carrying it through the back door. The other man, Flaco, shakes his head sadly as he looks on. Moments later Diablo returns soaked and wet from his shoulders to his waist.

Diablo is the leader of a small, but violent Latino street gang in Los Angles known as the Los Angles Aztecs. Flaco is his right-hand man and the large warehouse they are in is the gang's headquarters.

"I want another dog, Flaco! Get us a winner! I will not lose any more money! We are not losers!" Diablo demands, taking a towel from the bench and drying his hands and arms.

Flaco takes a deep breath, "Nobody is selling grand champs Diablo. Where will I find a dog that's a winner?" Flaco pleads.

Diablo looks at his second in command and smiles, "Then don't buy it!"

CHAPTER 15

Rich Jr. glances nervously around the interior of the large metal barn as Ron pulls alongside a white panel van. As he parks the Suburban and turns the ignition off Ron can sense the fear in the boy as he studies the faces of the men around. When the hum of the garage doors motor causes Rich Jr. to jump in his seat Ron knows it is time for a talk of encouragement.

"I'll stomp y'er damn ears together if you embarrass me! Stop looking like a cop at a convict convention! Act like a man!" Ron growls from behind his stained yellow teeth.

Rich Jr. attempts to compose himself as Ron wonders if he should have brought the boy to meet Vance so soon? The time would have to come but Ron is sure he jumped the gun but it is too late to go back now he decides.

The face nearest is that of a follower, not of a man who controls seventy percent of the drug trade in Atlanta. The guy watching the open door growing ever more closed is a soldier; maybe really good at what he does but only a soldier.

But number three; the sharp eyes of a seasoned convict the stance and jaw line of a brawler with an intellectual air about him. A man obviously more intelligent than himself, Rich Jr. decides.

"There he is!" Ron exclaims and as Rich Jr. follows his uncles eyes he sees a man in an expensive business suit enter a back door. As he comes into view it is painfully obvious to Rich Jr. how bad of a judge of character he actually is.

Nash Vance could be a car salesman, a lawyer or a politician. His hair had that personal barber sheen and wave. His walk was a strut of not just confidence but invincibility. Tanned skin with Ice cold blue piercing eyes, whiskey brown hair with gray at the temples, the kind of gray both very handsome and very wise men acquire in later years.

"Don't do nothin' stupid!" Ron sneers as he exits the truck. Rich Jr. attempts to catch up but Ron is already extending his hand to shake Vance's by the time he arrives. A suave City Socialite and the county swamp bumpkin, some sight the two make as they stand shaking hands.

"Ron, you mean old bastard, every year I think it is going to be the last time I see you and every year you just keep popping up...How the hell are you?" Vance flashes a campaign smile of sincerity as he makes it a two-handed shake taking the wrinkled blue veined hand of the old man's in both of his.

To Rich Jr's. shock, Ron returns the smile. It's a stained yellow worn toothed smile that compared to Vance's by brilliance and beauty, is actually disgusting. But, for a sheer rarity Rich Jr. cannot take his eyes off of the unique sight. "I'm doin' alright Nash and I see yer' still a dandy!" Ron's cordiality is so out of place that it is somewhat uncomfortable to Rich Jr.

Vance's eyes shift directly upon the boy as he steps up beside Ron. In a flash Vance's eyes flicker into a cold stare of calculation but within a couple of seconds the Ice blue eyes flip and they are the warm blue of a pilot light. Rich Jr. has the feeling of a man just measured and weighed in two seconds.

Nash extends his hand, and as the boy shakes it he feels a firm grip that seems to be restraining an almost threatening strength beneath the surface.
"That's the one that I'm trying to pass the torch off to." Ron explains.

Pulling his hand back. "It is nice to meet you Richard but we both know this old Eagle will more than likely out-live us both." with a salesman's flashy smile. Before glancing over Rich Jr's.' shoulder at the strong-jawed sentry.

With a glance from Vance the three guards begin vigorously unpacking the compacted packages of marijuana from the Suburban into the rear of the panel van.
Nash turns to Ron, his hand finding the old man's shoulder and not bitten off.

"Let's go to the office so I can show you the new bowling bag I got you."

Ron allows Vance to lead him into a small office where piles of old tires make a corridor on either side of the office entrance. Rich Jr. follows behind feeling like a fifth wheel.

In the tiny office, a black leather bowling ball bag sits upon a desk with chairs on either side. Vance leads the old man to one chair as Ron takes the bag from the desk and hands it back to Rich Jr.

"Take this out to my truck, wait for me, I'll be out soon. Ron doesn't turn as he talks to his nephew and the boy takes the bag out of the office and to his uncle's Suburban.

Seated in the passenger side of the old truck Rich Jr. feels as if this may not be the kind of life he can handle. Vance seems not to like him and the entire situation has him scared to death.

Out of boredom the boy opens the leather bag and begins counting the banded bills. His disposition begins changing as thousands become tens of thousands and there is still much left to count when the sound of Ron's coughing causes him to hastily stop tallying the bills and quickly stuff them back into the bag. Ron climbs in behind the wheel and slams the door shut without the slightest expression on his leathery scruffy face, as he waits for the garage door to open he looks over at his nephew in the passenger's seat and lights a cigarette.

"You gonna' be able to do this? You gonna' be able to handle this shit?" The old man exhales a cloud of smoke.

The money, as often happens, has allowed Rich Jr. to begin believing he is someone he isn't. "You're damn right I can!" The boy responds with a conviction that has convinced himself thoroughly but doesn't quite persuade Ron.

* * *

CHAPTER 16

Verez steps into her apartment, a grocery bag in her arms, and shuts the door with her foot as her cell phone begins to ring. She sets the bag on the kitchen counter and answers the call. "What's up Chuck?" she replies in her usual greeting.

"I heard you collected enough evidence to secure an indictment against seven of them, congratulations." He comments from the other end of the line. "Yeah, four months going into that old musty castle. It creeped me out to be surrounded by that many sleaze balls with a fifty foot wall keeping me locked in there with them." Verez begins placing food in the cupboards.

"It must have been pretty scary...how many of them were in there for violent crimes?" he asks. Verez stops with a carton of milk in her hand on the way to the refrigerator. "I don't know about the inmates...I was talking about the guards. They were worse than the inmates. I can't believe I only got seven indictments...federal prisons rotten with corrupt staff...it's unbelievable what goes on in that place!" Verez places the milk into the refrigerator.

"Well, I wanted to congratulate you and ask you if you're still interested in this guy...ah Vance something...Nash Vance...that's it...you remember him right?" Casey jokes. "You're damn right I'm interested! Do we have something new on him?" she asks as she folds the paper bag.

"Well, unless it's too good to be true, I think we might have one of Vance's low-level gophers?" he explains. Verez appears skeptical. "Yeah, we've been fooled before. Has he said anything to prove he's credible?" "Well he won't say too much right now, but he says if we can get him a time cut he'll give us one of Vance's drug connections. A guy Vance has been dealing with for over twenty years." Casey explains.

"A time cut? The guy's in prison? How much is he asking off?" Verez braces herself. The typical rule thirty-five (b)...fifty percent cut." He says sarcastically. "What the hell is he in for and how much time does he have?" bracing herself again.

"Child pornography and he got sixty months," Casey spits it out as if it's a ball of bile. "Jesus Christ A chomo? Sixty months? It's stuff like this that makes me wonder if I'm on the side of the good guys! Five years for being a pedophile?" Verez vents.

"I feel the same way Verez, but it's the system we work for. How bad do we want Vance? That's the real question!" he reasons. "Bad, but damn Chuck? Bad enough to put a sicko' back on the streets in half the time. I already considered a hundred years too little.

"I've already sent my request to the prosecutor's office. The guy's in a hurry because he scores maximum custody level points and he's on protective custody for the third time in seven months at his third United States penitentiary." Casey explains hoping that the suffering of the creep calms her. It does.

"Well, I'll come in first thing in the morning, and we'll discuss it then, but this low life better have something or I'll cut something alright. I'll cut it off and kick it around the floor." She snarls. "You're starting to creep me out Verez, you scary bitch," Casey is almost not joking.

"Well, I'll see you tomorrow boss." She walks into her living room. "Alright Verez, get some sleep and good job with the undercover work. You're a machine." He compliments before hanging up. Verez thinks about making a deal with a child sex offender and shivers.

Her apartment is Spartan; a single couch sits against the wall with a bare coffee table in front of it. On the wall opposite, a flat screen TV sits on a stand – plugs still coiled and unconnected to the wall outlet. There are no pictures on the walls and boxes fill a spare room, while her room holds only a queen size bed, a dresser and a night stand with a single lamp and alarm clock upon it. A holster hangs from the bed post she sleeps near, where she keeps her thirty-eight revolver at night.

Work is her life. Other than Chuck Casey, her cell phone has but six other numbers: four are directly work related, one is the bank and the other is a Chinese takeout restaurant that she has sworn off but keeps on her phone in case she relapses.

She accepted an invite from a few co-workers to go out for drinks, once when she did not want to be rude. She did not assault anyone or anything so bad, but by the evening's end, it was clear that she would not be invited or be accepting another invite, though all agreed they should do it again real soon.

She accepts the fact she is not a people person and work is the only thing that makes her feel complete. Only one other thing has ever compared, one other thing that, she was good at, and that was war.

She hasn't been in a relationship since college, and those situations ended because human contact felt too unnatural. She could never have someone stay overnight.

The nights are the worst. The flashbacks that sometimes occur during the day frequently happen at night as she sleeps. And as a result, she wakes, more nights than not, screaming and crying. It's always the same nightmare, her father being attacked and the dark man with the gun who breathes smoke like a devil. His face she cannot remember but the smoke she cannot forget. He haunts her, controls her and runs her life.

After all these years he is every bad guy she has fought, chased or arrested. He is her failure while still, at the same time, being the reason, she succeeds: her motivation and her nightmare. She will never face this demon, and so she may never conquer the fear.

This is her life, an empty two-bedroom apartment, a windowless mop closet of an office and murderers, drug pushers and corrupt officials, and last, but certainly not least, Nash Vance. She may never find the dark man, but she will never lose another. This she vows to herself and her father.

* * *

CHAPTER 17

As they pull back to the large barn, the crowd moves and allows Ron's Suburban to pull up to the open double doors. Rich Jr. gets out and walks to the back door of Ron's vehicle and almost trips over a young kid with a camera phone recording them.

Rich Jr. opens the Suburban's back door and takes hold of the Brindle's chain and leads him out of the truck and through the crowd in the packed barn. The people part and allow the dog and his two owners through.

A large, barrel-chested man in overalls walks up to Ron and shakes his hand. The man is Jack Dabois and he owns the barn and oversees the bets.

"How ya' doin', Ron? Some turnout, huh?" Jack looks around with a large smile on his face. Ron points at a support beam along the wall of the barn's side for Rich Jr. to secure the Brindle to, and his nephew chains the dog to it.

"There's talk that this dog is the one to beat yours, Ron, and a bunch of folks believing it too." Jack informs Ron.

Ron spits as he pulls a cigarette out. "Some folks would believe ya' if you told 'em it was rainin' while yer' pissin' on their shoes, but that don't make it so, Ain't nothin' besides a lion beating my dog Jack." Ron lights a cigarette as Jack points across the crowd.

"He ain't much less than a lion Ron." Ron follows his finger and sees the monster chained to a beam directly opposite of the Brindle. "They call 'em Hector and he's one-third pit bull, one third bull mastiff and one third Rottweiler. On top of that, they've been injecting the beast with steroids since its teeth busted through the gums. The breed is called 'pit bull killer' and they say he's never needed more than sixty seconds in the ring." Jack elaborates.

"Ron Arwood...the legend himself!" comes a voice from behind them. Ron turns to see a well-dressed man walking towards them with his hand extended. Ron takes the hand reluctantly. "Thomas Hopkins is the name. It's an honor to meet you, Ron." Hopkins greets him with a smile.

Ron throws his head towards the big black brute across the barn, "You the owner of that?"

"Yes, sir. Bill Mathenson trained him, but Hector's my dog," Hopkins beams proudly. "Sounds like you spent a good deal of money on 'em? That's a shame," Ron offers his condolences.

Hopkins laughs, "Confidence is good Ron, I like that, but confidence and delusions look a lot alike where it's pride talking. Hector will kill your dog, Ron. He's never needed more than sixty seconds," Hopkins warns.

Ron drops the cigarette on the ground and grinds it out with his boot. "Confident enough to put fifty thousand where my mouth is. You willin' to do the same, Tom?" Ron pushes his button.

"That's a mighty fine donation Ron, but I only brought twenty grand with me," Hopkins explains.

"I'll tell ya' what, Tom. I'll credit that shiny new black truck of yours. I believe it's yours I saw coming in? Ain't never seen it around here before? I'll credit it twenty-five grand!" Ron pushes still.
Flushed, Hopkins takes the bait.
"That's a two thousand fourteen Tahoe! It's worth forty thousand as is!"

"You don't sound so confident no more, Tom," Ron tickles the line. A wild look comes over Hopkins face.

"Alright old man. Alright, but I'm still five thousand short?" Hopkins swallows the bait, hook and all. Ron looks down at Hopkins' expensive boots.
"I'll give ya' five grand for them snake skin boots." Ron skins his catch. Hopkins looks down at his own boots.

"These are ostrich skin," he corrects.

"Hell, I don't care what kind of snake it is," Ron explains.

59

Across the barn, the Brindle has discovered a large cow bone but it's just beyond his reach as he strains his chain attempting to get it. Suddenly, it slides forward and he snatches it up. He rises with the bone in his mouth and meets the gaze of who pushed it to him. It's a large brown and white Saint Bernard.

Their eyes meet, and it's clear that neither feels any animosity towards the other. In fact, Rich Jr. thinks as he looks on, they seem to be friendly. Suddenly a raspy voice calls out.

"Sambo! Get away from that dog!" an old man, Sam Ball, runs over and pulls his big clumsy saint Bernard away from the Brindle. "I told you stay away from them monsters. They's dangerous ya' big dummy!" He explains to his dog as he leads him through the crowd.

"All of ya' listen up now! Hey! Listen up! Ya' got five minutes before I close the bets! Blue tickets are Arwood's Brindle and the red ones are Hopkins' dog! If you don't run your bets through me then I can't make sure you get paid! Side bets are not my responsibility!" Jack exclaims as he yells over the crowd noise. Over two hundred men pack the barn, but his booming voice reaches the furthest corners.

Tickets are being passed around, and Ron notices that the red outnumber the blue by at least four to one. "Hey, Unc', them boys from North Carolina are walking around in the crowd showing people some of Hector's past fights on these little DVD's. They say he's never been in the pit more than sixty seconds. Rich Jr. appears worried as he looks across at Hector who stalks back and forth on his chain like a caged tiger waiting for its meal. He looks at the Brindle and sees the dog chewing on a bone, not a care in the world.

Ron walks to his nephew. "Take the fifty thousand in the compartment in the truck and give it to Jack and put it on the Brindle," Ron winks. Rich Jr. is shocked.

"You already bet that money with the Tom guy? What if we lose, Unc'?"

"If we don't win it means the barn must have collapsed and killed us all anyway. So, what's it matter? Nothin' else is gonna save that dog." Ron says completely confident. Rich Jr. starts to go to the truck when a high-pitched yelp and a deep throated growl cause's the crowd to go silent. When they part, Rich Jr. and Ron see what the noise was.

Hector drops the lifeless body of the gentle Sambo to the ground. "He killed 'em in the blink of an eye!" One spectator yells suddenly many blue tickets are moving toward the chalkboard where Jack Dabois stands and replaces them with red ones.

Rich Jr. looks at the Brindle who stands, bone at his paws, looking intently across the barn at Hector who stands proudly over the lifeless body of the old Saint Bernard Sambo.

"Go get the money fool! Look at the Brindle! That's the look I was tellin' you about...that's hate boy...that's a killer!" Ron exclaims.

Rich Jr. dashes to Ron's truck and then a loud cry is heard. "Oh Sambo! He killed 'em! Dammit Sambo!" Sam Ball cries out heartbroken.

A woman comes and comforts Sam as two young boys with a wheel barrel take the body away. Rich Jr. takes the bag to Jack who looks up at Ron for confirmation. Ron nods and Jack, with a look of concern, hands the bag to his bet takers and says something to the man. Jack pulls a red ticket from his own pocket, looks at Ron as if to say, 'Are you sure?' Ron nods his head again and with faith Jack changes the house's bet from red to a blue ticket. His bet taker protests but Jack overrides his opinion.

Jack steps up on a large crate and puts his hands around his mouth. "Alright! Let's get 'em in! If you're going to change your bets get 'em in now because this is last call!" Jack looks at the last few red tickets being handed out and puts his hand back to his mouth. "Alright! That's it! No more."

"Wait! Wait Jack! I want to bet!" A raspy voice calls from the crowd. Jack scans the faces and sees Sam Ball making his way to the booth.

"Sam? Sam, you ain't ever bet on a fight in your life?" Jack yells. Sam gets to Jack. "I am now! I'm bettin' the farm on Arwood's Brindle!" Sam Ball demands.

"All you have is an old truck and a trailer Sam! You don't have any money!" Jack reasons.

"I own the four acres that trailer sits on! I'll bet it all right now against fifty grand with any man who wants to bet." Sam looks around at the men.

"Somebody take this fool's money. While the getting's good!" yells Hopkins, whose entourage all laugh.

One of Hopkins' men steps up. "I got a bass boat and twenty grand!" He smirks.

"It's a bet!" Sam Ball accepts.

Jack Dabois attempts to stop Sam from betting. "You're betting with your heart Sam, dammit! Don't do this!" Sam won't hear it.

The other man and Sam step to Jack who finalizes the bet and looks past them at Ron who just winks. Ten minutes later the crowd encircles the ring which is an area about fifteen feet long and ten feet wide, walled in by a double row of square hay bales. At one end of the pit Hector strains his chain so much that his collar is choking him and his breathing can be heard scrapping his wind pipe as the collar presses against his trachea.

Fifteen feet away, across from him, the Brindle stands calmly looking straight ahead at his eager opponent. Hector is forty pounds larger and nearly a foot taller and there is a look of want in the big brute's eyes, a want to inflict pain, a want to taste blood and a want to bring death.

Just before the collars are broken, a silence falls over the two hundred plus men like calm before the coming storm. Then suddenly the collars break and thunder crashes as Hector races across the pit. The Brindle not only stays in place but does something that causes Ron's heart to skip a beat. The Brindle stands high, on front paws, and offers his throat, as he looks to the barn ceiling with his head raised.

Suicide! He's committing' suicide! Ron thinks as Hector rushes forward. It's over! That is the thought of every man seeing the spectacle in the ring. Sam Ball closes his eyes. Jack Dabois turns away. Thomas Hopkins screams in delight and Ron Arwood growls with rage.

Hector reaches the Brindle, head turned, massive jaws agape. He bites down on the exposed throat of his doomed foe intent on ripping his neck open, but only too late does Hector realize his mistake as his powerful jaws snap shut on empty air followed by a vice fitted with spikes closing upon his own, carelessly exposed throat.

The Brindle witnessed Hector's attack on Sambo, the large Saint Bernard, and it angered him, he saw Hector's Achilles heel. The brute attacks so confidently that he disregards the precautions that fighting dogs must remember. The throat is every dog's weakness and even when attacking it must be protected. Hector fears no dog, but he also respects no dog – hence his final mistake, for the Brindle demands respect.

As Hector blindly rushes in, the Brindle at the last moment, drops to his left, straight down, and comes up from below the lunging monster with the unprotected throat as Hector is lifted off his feet and flipped backward. There is yet again a look of want in his eyes, a want of air, a want of mercy and a want to be back home beneath the Dogwood tree in North Carolina because he knows this is not where he belongs.

Nothing Hector has wanted happens this day. He does not taste blood. The only death and destruction will be his own and in this pit he will find no air or mercy, and he will never leave southern Georgia. As he is slammed to his back, the Brindle literally begins mopping the floor with the larger animal. A stream of urine sprays between Hector's legs to land in the faces of Hopkins and his entourage. Men watch fortunes won and lost. Hector's record of never being in the ring more than sixty seconds remains unbroken.

In the crowd, a young man records it all on his camera phone and though he doesn't know it, he and his phone will change the courses of many lives.

A half hour later, Rich Jr. drives his uncle's Suburban away from the barn. Ron, behind the wheel of Hopkins' Tahoe, stops in front of Thomas Hopkins. "Nice doing business with ya' Tom!" Ron gloats from the open window. "Go to hell Arwood!" Hopkins demands as Ron looks down at Hopkins' feet. "Nice socks Tom!" Ron laughs as he drives away. Hopkins looks down at his shoeless feet and curses.

CHAPTER 18

Northern Los Angles, California

Jasmine stands looking out of her classroom window as several birds take baths outside in the soft brown dirt beneath the swings. Behind her, the other children sing 'Mary had a Little Lamb' and Jasmine appears to hear nothing. Through the glass of the class door, Sarah and the principal, watch Jasmine from the school hallway.

"Have you tried to get her involved in any of the class activities?" Sarah asks. The principal, Judy Orwitz, nods her head.

"You know we have, Sarah. Jasmine is in her own world. She colors and plays with blocks and seems to like stuffed animals, but she has no interest in being part of the group," Mrs. Orwitz explains.

"She looks so unhappy all the time. Look at her?" Sarah watches her daughter.

"She's not unhappy Sarah; I'd say that she is very happy. Jasmine is not the first Autistic child we've had here. They may never laugh or smile and seem completely uninterested in anything, but that doesn't make it true. We've watched them; we've watched her when nobody else is around. She finds all sorts of things to do, but it's like she doesn't want anyone around when she plays with her dolls or the blocks. She may never laugh or smile, but it doesn't mean she isn't happy. She's just in a world of her own and won't come into ours. Nothing out here interests her," Mrs. Orwitz comforts.

Sarah looks at Jasmine, who appears to stare blindly out of the classroom window, "I never thought about it...I don't know how, but I've never really thought about that? I've never heard her laugh. I've never seen her smile. I...I don't even know if she can?" Sarah wonders.

CHAPTER 19

East Los Angles, California

Diablo sits in his dark office, the only lights coming from his computer monitor illuminating his face. There is a knock on the door before it opens slowly. Flaco peaks his head inside, "You wanted me Diablo?" he asks.

"Yes, come in. There is something I want you to see. I wanted it to be a surprise, but I can't wait any longer," the gang lord confesses with a child-like enthusiasm which is completely out of his character, Flaco thinks, and looks around the dark office suspiciously as he enters. He walks slowly around the desk.

Diablo points to the screen while hitting the play button as Falco begins watching.

"Why the hell is he doing that...oh, shit!" Falco's eyes grow huge. Diablo watches his second in command's face and laughs.

"Huh? What the hell do you think about that? Diablo turns to Falco. Flaco shakes his head in disbelief and stares at the paused scene on the monitor.

"That's a bad-assed dog, homes," Flaco declares.

"Damned right he is, and he's going to be our bad ass dog," Diablo smiles proudly.

How? Flaco wonders, not taking his eyes off the monster.

"I sent two brothers to get him two days ago. I kept it quiet, but I couldn't keep it from you anymore," Diablo explains.

"How do you know where he is?" Flaco asks. Diablo rewinds the footage further to the Brindle being taken from the back of the Suburban and pauses it. He looks up at Flaco.

Flaco appears confused. "How does that tell us where he is?" Flaco remains baffled.

"The license plate, Loco." Diablo points out. Flaco nods his head but still appears puzzled. "I had one of our people who works at the DMV run the plates. The dude's name is Ronald Arwood and he lives in southern Georgia. I Google earthed it, and the dude's in the swamp," Diablo explains.

"He will sell us the dog?" Flaco can't believe it.

"I don't know if it's for sale? Who cares, we are not buying it. Mi plomo por tu perro." Diablo smirks.

CHAPTER 20

Casey and Verez wait in a room between two huge metal sliding doors. Large bulletproof windows run the length of one wall of the room. The control center and a single guard are on the other side of the glass. The guard acts as if they are not there as he watches a talk show on one of the monitors.

"What the hell is taking so long?" Casey looks at his watch.

"They are sending either a seasoned guard or a higher-ranking staff member to escort us. A younger officer or rookie might tell us something they don't want us to know." Verez informs him. Casey shakes his head.

"Not all prisons are as underhanded as Atlanta, Verez. They are not all the same," he assures her.

"Well, after what I saw, I don't trust any of them. We'll know when the escort is close. That talk show will flip to show footage from one of the prison cameras like the other monitors," Verez guesses.

Casey smirks and watches the monitor with the talk show on it. He begins to tell Verez about her stereotyping when he sees the guard change the monitor to a prison camera. The metal door ahead of them opens and a bald-headed man, with a bright white shirt and Lieutenant's bars on his lapel, looks them over suspiciously.

"Agent Verez, Charles Casey. I'm Lieutenant Boles," Baldy introduces himself. He turns as Casey starts to offer his hand and walks down the hall. Casey looks at Verez who raises her eyebrows as if to say, "I told you."

"I'll take you to the contact visitation room for our SHU inmates," Baldy says over his shoulder.

"Shoe inmates? Like tennis shoes, shoe?" Casey asks.

"No, it's S.H.U., Special Housing Unit. It's where disciplinary and protective custody inmates are held from general population inmates," Verez informs her boss.

Baldy turns toward her as he walks. "You worked a prison before?" Baldy asks half smiling. Casey closes his eyes bracing himself.

"For four months at U.S.P. Atlanta," she says. Thank God! Casey thinks to himself.

"Oh yeah? What happened did you quit?" Baldy appears more comfortable. Casey shakes his head.

"No, the investigation ended," Verez says. Casey feels as if he's dodging bowling balls.

"Investigation?" the guard asks, and Casey knows his luck is out.

"Yeah, I busted seven crooked guards who are now facing twenty years each," she says. Baldy stiffens and faces forward as he walks. Verez smirks. He leads them through a series of sliding doors until they come to a room with large bulletproof windows. The room is small with a table and a few chairs.

In one of the chairs, a man sits. He is in a bright orange jumpsuit. Baldy says nothing as he lets them in the room and shuts the door behind them. "I'm Charles Casey and this is Agent Verez," Casey says. Joey Babbs extends his hand to Casey who hesitates before shaking it. When Babbs offers his hand to Verez, she pretends to search her pockets for something. Once she sees that his hand remains, she gives up the charade and looks directly at him. Casey sees another bowling ball coming.

"I'm not shaking your hand," she says with a false smile. Verez sees fresh pink scars on his face and a hint of yellow above both cheeks below his healing black eyes, Babbs begins to say something, but the look in her eyes shuts him down.

"What do you have for us, Mr. Babbs?" Casey asks attempting to cut through the tension.

"I...I want something in writing first," he demands. Casey reaches into his inside jacket pocket and produces an envelope. He hands it to Babbs, who opens it and reads the document.

"It's been signed by your attorney and the prosecutor. You'll have thirty months shaved off of your sentence." Casey promises. Verez clinches her teeth as Babbs' eyes brighten, and a smile spreads across his battered face.

"I'll be out in two and a half months," he says and his body appears to relax.

"That's only if you have information leading to the arrest of Nash Vance," Casey warns.

Babbs sits back with an arrogant smile. "What I got will put Vance away alright, but it's up to you to catch him in the act and to do that it's not Vance you need to get first, it's his supplier," Babbs extends his legs and relaxes.

"Well, who is his supplier? And what's he supplying?" Casey rests his elbows on the table.

"The guy delivers the product to Forest Park in Clayton County where it's hidden in a safe house. Vance has quantities delivered to locations all around the city in Atlanta, and the guy only brings the product once a year, five hundred pounds per load."

Verez and Casey look at each other. Casey leans forward, "So what's the product?" he asks.

"The guy makes the best...Vance has been dealing with him for twenty years or better and the city loves it, but the guy will only deliver five hundred pounds a year. Vance won't stop dealing with the guy because it's high grade and better than anyone else can..."

"Alright Dickhead! Enough with the riddles. You have your deal creep, give us some names and real answers or I'll stuff that deal down your throat!" Verez stares at him as if he's a cockroach she wishes to crush.

Babbs swallows, looks at Casey and sees he's not playing the good cop role and so doubts Verez is playing the bad cop. She does not appear to be playing at all, he thinks. "It's marijuana and the guy's..."

"Marijuana! You little punk chomo! What the hell..." Verez interrupts before being interrupted by Casey.

"Verez! Let's step out of the room for a moment," Casey intervenes.

Babbs appears very scared as they step into the hall and close the door. "Pot isn't going to get Vance anytime! Hell, the supplier will get more time than Vance!" Verez protests.

"I agree Verez, but it's something," Casey explains.

"No, no it's nothing. If it was cocaine, heroin, meth or ecstasy, then it would be something," she argues.

"No, it's not a boatload of time, but it's a search warrant. A way into Vance's fortress of secrecy that we've not been able to breach for years Verez, and this is the closest we've been. This is the best shot we have at getting him. Al Capone was destroyed by being busted for tax evasion. It was the least of his crimes, but it was the thread that unraveled his entire empire," Casey preaches.

"Alright, I get it, I just don't like this little Chomo," she confesses. Casey looks at her. "What's a Chomo?" he asks. "It's a child molester. I heard it at the prison in Atlanta," she smiles.

In the room, Babbs is still nervous, and Casey gives him a moment to wonder if Verez is going to be allowed to attack him before he questions him any further. "Alright, so the guy brings Vance five hundred pounds of marijuana. How much is the bill?" he asks.

"Five hundred a pound for it all. Two hundred and fifty grand in bulk." he answers, periodically shifting his gaze to Verez, as if expecting her to snap any moment. Casey notices the answers Babbs now gives are straight to the point.

"Well, what's the supplier's name? Casey asks.

"He's like a hundred years old and lives out in the..." Babbs sees Verez shift in her   seat,   "Arwood...Ron   Arwood."

CHAPTER 21

From behind the safety and anonymity of the limousine tinted windows a man watches as Casey and Verez exit the prison and make their way to their vehicle in the penitentiary parking lot.

He removes a cell phone from his jacket pocket and speed dials a number as he keeps his eyes on the two federal officers.

After two rings a man's voice answers on the other end.

"So, what's going on now?" Nash Vance asks calmly from the comfort of his downtown Atlanta office.

"They've just left the prison... An hour and a half inside... I'd say he's talking." The man in the sedan surmises, not taking his eyes from the federal vehicle pulling out of the parking area.

"God-damned it, I told you I wanted that little weasel dead! What the hell did I pay those losers for? Not to just rough him up! Why the hell is Babbs still alive?" Vance growls into the receiver.

"I did just as you said. How the hell was I to know those pussies would not get it done? They are both doing life. I can do it myself when he gets out. I'll know it's done right..."

"A lot of fucking good it will do me when I'm in there instead of him, Asshole!" Vance cuts into his henchman.

"What do you want me to do? How can I fix this?" The squared jaw man asks.

After a moment's pause to calm himself Vance makes a decision. "Maybe it's time to be even more pro-active. We've been getting rid of witnesses but every time this bitch finds another... Make sure she can't find another one... Ever." The line goes dead with Vance's last words.

He has killed several times in the employ of Nash Vance, and a few times before that working as a soldier of fortune in the west of Africa and the jungles of Brazil. Politicians, Cartel members and other S.O.F.'s. In rare occasions a few have had to be women and, though he did not particularly like killing woman, it always made the act worse when using a weapon. Something about killing a woman seemed amoral unless it was done with his hands.

"It's more intimate, more righteous, done with my hands." He's always told himself. He focuses on his hands while steering the sedan out of the prison parking lot.

CHAPTER 22

A gym night. He has watched her return to her apartment many times over the last couple of years and has noticed that she is a true creature of habit She picks up only a small amount of groceries on her way home from work a few nights a week. The only time the chrome revolvers not in the holster on the right side of her waist is when she's returning from the gym. Then and only then it is in her gym bag.

Odd, he thinks, that she should break protocol and carry a revolver when the federally issued sidearm happens to be a Sig, .45. It's one of the many things he admires about her. Admiration and respect can still be felt towards someone he intends to kill, that's been the way a few times in the past and it is so now.

He knew that even though she had had such a long day on the road to Atlanta from Kentucky that she would still go to the gym as she did every Tuesday and Sunday evening.

On these nights, with the gun in her bag, it would be much easier to take her without having to worry about the revolver in the equation. He had initially planned on getting her as she exited her S.U.V. but the rain and howling wind of the thunderstorm gave way to another, even better, option.

Seeking temporary shelter from the wind and rain he found the ideal location for the kill. Her apartment sat at the end of the corridor on the third floor of the building and across from her door an alcove deep enough for him to be concealed in the shadows existed. Shadows provided by the slight un-screwing of a seventy-five-watt bulb with a few twists of his gloved hand as it rested in its socket.

The torrential down-pour, howling wind and sound of thousands of vehicles from the inner-state just on the other-side of a small grove of pine trees just behind the complex makes for great cover noise should something go wrong and she's somehow able to scream out. He knows though that nothing will go wrong as he settles into his ambush spot and begins the exercise that has made him such a successful killer all these years.

He sees her as she walks to her door, steps and drops the gym bag before finding the key and sliding it into the lock. She opens it and bends down and grabs the bag and stands up as he wraps one arm quickly around her tiny neck and brings her into his embrace, lifting her off her feet in one swift motion. He feels her nails dig helplessly into his muscled arms as she struggles and kicks futilely until her little body goes still and limp in his arms.

Quick and simple he thinks as a clap of thunder brings him out of his visualization of the kill to come. He knows it's his uncanny ability to imagine the kill in all its details and intricacies, that has given him so much success through the years. Over and over he plays it in his head, playing and re-playing so that he can imagine, foresee and over-come any and all possible scenarios that may arise. It must be quick, efficient, silent and uneventful.

Its nearly a half hour before he hears the unmistakable sounds of shoes on concrete coming up the corridor towards his position. Even through the raging storm he can hear her on the way towards him as he calms himself for the kill to come.

She enters his field of vision as she arrives at her door. The bag is in her left hand, she does not drop it as she slides the key into the lock with her right hand. He moves, silent and wraith-like, from the shadows and, just as he envisioned, his arm wraps expertly around her tiny little neck. In one swift motion he pulls her into his embrace and lifts her off her feet.

Its not his muscled arm that he feels her nails sink into but rather the center of his left testicle through the thin material of his grey slacks, she crushes it so furiously that he is forced to release her as he nearly blacks out from the pain.

As he releases her, he propels her to the door intending on continuing the attack but is shocked when a foot digs into his solar plexus and the wind is knocked from him. Through blurry eyes he sees her attempt to shake off the effects of the strangle hold meant to be the end of her.

She drops down and begins reaching into the bag and he attacks her once more before she can pull her hand from the bag. His momentum has sent her to the concrete floor, and him on top of her keeps her from being able to remove her hand from the bag as he begins to strangle her with both of his gloved hands.

He looks into her dark eyes and begins to strangle the life from her but it's not fear that he finds in them but something else. As he increases the force around her throat her secret is revealed brutally to him.

His guts are rocked as a .357 slug explodes from the bag, and into his intestines tearing through his liver stopping between his hip and spine. A second slug perforates his kidney before exiting his back and a third pierces his stomach, severs his spine and has only enough momentum to drop a foot and a half away upon Verez's door mat.

As the darkness embraces him he can think but one small but all-consuming thought, "What just happened?"

CHAPTER 23

Ron sits at the kitchen table beneath his usual cloud of cigarette smoke. The house is silent, save for the tick of the clock on the wall beside the backdoor. Three days ago, he sent Rich Jr. to Waycross to sell the Tahoe they won and Rich Jr. had still not returned.

The boy did good posting the advertisement on the interweb Craigspace, Ron thinks, but every time he does one thing right, he screws two things up. Ron puts the cigarette out and begins to light another when a familiar sound is heard.

He hopes the girl isn't back. He had to tolerate the tart because the boy needed someone to follow him to the city in his truck, but he told the boy not to make it a habit of bringing her, or anyone else around. The truck's engine shuts off and Ron hears the sound of a door closing.

Just one. That's good news. He thinks and hears the sound of his nephew talking. Ron knows it isn't him on his mobile phone because it "couldn't get bars out this way." Whatever that means. He waits for a woman's voice, but only hears his nephew again and after a few moments the door opens and Rich Jr. enters wearing his sunglasses on the top of his head. Ron thinks he looks like a jackass.

"Damn, Unc', when I left a couple of days ago you was sittin' right there. You ever get out? Go to town or somewhere?" Rich Jr. asks before entering his room.

"I ain't went nowhere in the four years your stupid ass has been livin' here have I? I'm headin' towards eighty-year-old. I reckin' the only place I'm ever gonna go is hell. Speaking of it, where in the hell you been for three damn days and who's outside waitin' on ya?" Ron asks.

"Nobody's outside waiting on me? What the hell are you talkin' about? Anyway, I was at Kristine's uncle's pool hall. In the back room, he lets people gamble for money on real poker machines. You ought to try it sometime, Unc'! A lot of older people are in there playing those things," Rich Jr. calls from his room.

"I ain't messin' with no poker machines. Anything that backs its ass up against the wall and challenges the world's gotta be bad enough to get the best of me."

Rich Jr. explodes in laughter in his room, and Ron waits for his nephew's chuckles to subside before he continues. "You explain stuff in the darnest ways, Unc'," Rich Jr. says coming into the kitchen.

"The hell with that! Who the hell's out front? Who was you talking to? Don't tell me you wasn't because I heard ya! I told you about havin' people here!" Ron accuses.

Rich Jr. looks baffled before he smiles and nods his head. "Oh yeah, no it's not any person, Unc'. There's a beagle dog out front. I couldn't get 'em to come out from under your truck though," he explains.

"Why don't you feed Sugar, it's your job to feed the dogs and she ain't ate in three damn days," Ron stands up.

"Why didn't you feed her if you fed Black and Brindle?" he asks his uncle who is walking towards the front door cutting a piece of jerky he pulled from his coverall pockets.

"I didn't feed 'em. Black dug into the pen next to 'em. The one with that long hornets' nest in it and ate the nest." Ron opens the door.

"He ate a hornets' nest?" Rich Jr. grimaces.

"The poor bastard...his head looks like a sack of apples...all the stings he got." Ron starts through the door.

"You fed the Brindle though?" he asks the old man.

"Nope, but I'm about to," Ron closes the door.

Ten minutes later Rich Jr. has just finished feedin' Sugar when he sees his uncle carrying a beagle. "You gonna keep it, Unc'?" he asks walking with the old man toward the back of the property.

"Hell no! Ain't no dog worth havin' 'cept a pit bull," Ron spits as he continues. "What in hell are you doin' with 'em then?" he asks the old man.

"Feeding the Brindle dummy," his uncle answers matter of fact like.

Rich Jr. stops walking for a moment, but Ron seems not to notice as he continues toward the Brindle's large pen in the very back. Rich Jr. runs to catch up and arrives just as Ron drops the beagle dog over the fence of the pen. The small dog is young and very energetic as it jumps up playfully attempting to get back up into Ron's arms, oblivious to the danger that it is in.

The little dog barks playfully as it leaps up enjoying the attention of the two men. It's not until the sound of chains rattling and blocks sliding over concrete that he turns around to see the violent end of his life moving towards him. A sharp cry escapes the helpless hound as he drops to his back and whimpers, submissively licking the nose of the killer that looms over him collecting the scent of his terror and innocence.

The beagle's body quivers in anticipation of the brutal attack that he just knows is coming. The Brindle smells the helpless creature, not as an opponent or a threat or even a meal to quiet the hunger he has felt for days; he smells him in an attempt to understand why the small dog smells like other dogs have been around him he's not a dog for fighting? He also carries the scent of people...several different human scents, scents the Brindle has never smelled before.

"Eat 'em or you ain't getting' nothing else you weak bastard!" Ron demands from the other side of the fence. The Brindle takes a few more deep smells of the beagle. The scents make him feel strange, warm inside, so good it almost hurts...then he turns dragging his burden of fourteen cinder blocks away with him as he goes.

"He's showing the little fella mercy, Unc'," Rich Jr. says as Ron reaches down and grabs the beagle who leaps thankfully into the old man's arms. The dog licks his face in gratitude.

"He didn't show Hector no mercy!" Ron pushes the beagle's head away from his own. "Hector was a killer. That's a beagle and nearly a puppy. He ain't a threat," Rich Jr. laughs as Ron tries to keep the small hound from licking his face.

"Well, let's see how much mercy ol' Black shows the little rat bastard."

Ron takes the small dog to Black's pen and tosses him over the fence. Rich Jr. turns away, but not before seeing Black catch the animal midair. He can't help but hear the sharp cry of pain and the violent cracking of bones before the sickening sounds of silence ends it all. Ron walks around the front of the house, and Rich Jr. makes sure the old man is out of sight before he sneaks to the barn for a self-medicated break.

CHAPTER 24

Ron walks around the house, intent on taking the uncomfortable ostrich skin boots he won from Hopkins off and relaxing in his rocking chair. Instead, he finds two heavily tattooed Hispanic men getting out of a blue panel van in his driveway.

"If yer' lookin' for a beagle? I fed 'em to my pit bull, and I'll do the same to your brown asses if you don't get off my property! I ain't got no oranges or 'maters need pickin' so get the hell out of here!" The old man snarls. The two men look at each other.

In the barn, Rich Jr. is sitting on the rafter, legs swinging, smoking a joint. More than a thousand marijuana plants hang upside down drying. Hearing his uncle cursing, he crushes the joint out and looks through the space between the wall boards and is shocked to see two Hispanic men dragging Ron, nose busted and lips bleeding, past the barn towards Black's pen.

Rich Jr. has never seen the men before, but the taller one holds a .45 in his right hand and Ron's shirt collar in the other. "Get that one first," the Aztec says to the short stocky one. Rich Jr. can see tattoos on both of their necks that are exactly alike.

"Diablo never said anything about a black one. He said to get the Brindle colored dog," the short Aztec argues.

"Look at him, he's a warrior. Two are better than one!" the taller man reasons before the other walks towards Black's pen.

"What the hell you wetbacks want? Who sent you?" Ron asks from his knees.

"Shut up you old redneck, and I might not kill you!" the Aztec yanks on his collar.

"Be careful. Get that rope hanging there and throw it around his neck first, then lead him out of the cage," the tall Aztec warns the other. Ron's eyes meet Rich Jr.'s and he shakes his head.

"Hey, it's cool, look at his tail wag, he's people friendly. Look at him, what the hell's wrong with his head? It looks like someone beat on 'em with a hammer. There's knots all over..." the Aztec screams as Black jumps up and bites down on his arm.

It's not malice or rage that Black feels as he attacks but rather a deep seeded desire to extinguish energy, to crush the writhing squealing into motionless silence. He savors the wringing of the electric pulses that he can feel racing between his jaws as the man's heart beats like the pinnacle of a crescendo. It's not violent at all, it is the joy of a puppy with a play toy, for in Black's tormented existence, and he has found joy, as every living thing must, in the snubbing out of life. Black has only the joy of the kill to look forward to in his poor miserable life. The nub wags away.

"Shoot him! Shoot it!" he yells as the dog lets go to get a better grip higher up on the arm!

"That-a-boy, Black! You like Mexican don't ya' boy?" Ron laughs as the other Aztec looks for a clear shot. Black turns loose and grips higher up the arm making his way closer to his victim's throat, but before he can reposition, a shot rings out. Black escapes through the bushes and out into the swamp beyond.

"Ol' Black ruined your orange picking career, Paco! Ha, Ha, Ha!" Ron laughs.

The tall Aztec walks over to Ron and without hesitation, fires four shots that throw him back and to the ground. He is dead before the third and fourth bullet strike him in the chest. Rich Jr. nearly falls off the rafter and holds his breath for fear of being discovered.

The tall Aztec takes his shirt off and rips it to wrap around the other's arm and for a moment they disappear from Rich Jr.'s view. When they do walk back by, they have the Brindle on his chain as they pass. The dog walks past Ron's body and only gives it a second glance before he and the murderers move out of Rich Jr.'s sight once more.

He waits for quite some time before dropping down to the barn floor and exiting. He walks to his uncle and finds the body cold and his eyes dry, open and milky. He did not love the man, won't cry for him, but he's saddened by the mean old bastard's death.

When Rich Jr.'s gets around to the front of the house, he finds the vehicle's engines all sabotaged. Spark plug wires are ripped out, and tires are slashed. Rich Jr. pulls out his cell phone to find it useless. "Dammit, no bars!" he stuffs the phone back into his pocket and starts to walk down the drive. He shakes his head and begins walking to the backyard.

* * *

CHAPTER 25

Black hobbles around a large bush on the edge of a lily covered pool of water. His left hind leg is injured. Though the bullet missed the bone, it ripped through the tight muscles of the leg and cut through a tendon. The leg drags uselessly across the ground as the dog moves on. He pants in the heat of the autumn swamp and just as he climbs over a downed log beside a pool, an eight-foot alligator crawls up the shore directly in his path.

The dog, despite living his entire life in the swamp, has never been face to face with an alligator. The gator sees the dog and has never seen a dog before, but the coldest months are ahead and whatever the black animal is, will have to do. The alligator opens his mouth wide and hisses. Black's head cocks to the side and his tail begins wagging.

* * *

CHAPTER 26

As Verez drives through the willow branches, she sees several county patrol cars, one unmarked Crown Victoria, a Coroner's car, and an ambulance in front of a small house on stilts. When she gets out of her Suburban, she sees a body being loaded into the ambulance.

"Agent Verez?" asks a large man with a cowboy hat and a Sheriff's badge pinned to his chest.

"Yes. What happened here?" she asks looking up at a billowing cloud of smoke rising high into the sky from the backyard.

"From our only witness' account, it was a murder, theft, and arson. Oh, and by the way, I'm Sheriff Matt Kenny," he extends his hand, and she shakes it. "Your boss...ah, Chuck Casey, said that you were on your way, but he wouldn't explain why the FBI was so interested in a state matter like this? As far as I can tell, it's a simple homicide, and it's not on the Okefenokee?" the Sheriff questions.

Verez's nose crinkles as she picked up an unmistakable scent in the air. The Sheriff looks at the smoke. "That seems to be the only reason you guys would be interested and the only thing left of a barn filled to bursting, I'd guess, with pot plants is a smoldering pile of ashes, hence the arson," the Sheriff smiles.

"I'd like to speak to the witness, if I could?" Verez looks around.

The Sheriff turns back to a young man sitting on the steps of the house. "Hey, Richie! Come here for a minute," the sheriff calls. The man stands up and walks over to them.

"Yeah, what's up Matt?" the man asks.

"This here's Special Agent Verez. She's with the FBI, and she needs to ask you a couple of questions. Tell 'er what you told us," he instructs the young man. The witness looks at Verez, seems nervous, but does as he's told.

"Well, I was in the barn when two Mexicans drug Unc', I mean Uncle Ron, over to Black's pen. The one fella' tries to get Black, but Ol' Black got 'em and I think the other guy shot Black because Black turned loose of the other guy and ran off into the swamp. Well, the guy with the gun shoots Unc', my uncle, before they both go and get the Brindle and take off! Rich Jr. explains.

Verez's eyebrows furrow. "So, you are in the barn watching this all?" she asks.

"Yeah, I was looking through the wall boards," he elaborates.

"Did you know the two men? Have you ever seen them before?" Verez looks around at the officers. It seems none are in a hurry to collect evidence.

"No, we don't have many Mexicans out here. No offense ma'am but we don't," he answers. "Did they have any scars, tattoos or distinctive features that you can recall?" Verez probes.

Rich Jr. stiffens for a moment. "Yeah, they both had lots of tattoos, but they both had the same tattoo on their neck. They were some sort of words, and they were exactly alike," he explains.

"Like Chinese letters or old English?" Verez asks.

"No, they were regular American letters but not American words? They spelled some strange words...like, "M." "I." "P" "L" "O" "M" "O'."

"Wait a minute, Verez interrupts him. "Mi plomo por tu plata" she says suspiciously.

Rich Jr. closes his eyes visualizing what he can remember. His lips silently spell out what he's seeing, and Verez realizes before he does, that she is correct. "Yeah, yeah, I think it was!" Rich Jr. confirms. Verez looks at the Sheriff.

"Can we go someplace private...just the three of us?" Verez asks.

Five minutes later they are sitting at the kitchen table inside Rich Jr.'s inherited home. Verez's cell phone has been placed in the center of the table. "How does your phone pick up out here, when no other phone will?" Rich Jr. asks trying his phone without success.

"It's an Agency phone," Verez responds.

"So, what you are saying is, a Los Angeles Street Gang, the Aztecs, sent two soldiers all the way across the country to kill an old man, steal his dog and burn his barn down?" Casey asks over the phone on the table.

"There is only one Gang that has that motto, and I've never heard of them having copycats or of ever branching out away from Los Angeles." Verez speaks to the phone.

"You think they did this for their own reason?" Casey asks. Verez shakes her head.

"I can't see the paths of this old man and them ever crossing. I think it's more likely a well-traveled and well-connected party decided to use some out of town talent to tie up a loose end. He must have learned about our prison visit last week?" Verez guesses.

"So, you think Nash Vance had them kill Arwood?" Casey asks. "Mr. Vance wouldn't hurt Unc'! They're friends! They've known each other for," Rich Jr. explains before he realizes he's said too much.

"You know Vance? You've been with your uncle when he's made the deliveries! You've been there when they made the transaction!" Verez accuses standing up.

"I don't know what you're talkin' about!" Rich Jr. looks nervously between her, the phone, and Sheriff Kenny.

"Yeah, like the Aztecs burnt down the barn, right? You left that part out of the story you told me! How'd you get out if they fired it with you inside? You set it on fire when you realized you had to call the cops, you little punk bitch!"

Verez starts to walk around to Rich Jr.'s side of the table. Casey repeatedly yells Verez's name on the conference call. When she finally hears him, she pauses as if deciding between him and Rich Jr. she decides and picks the phone up.

"Yes!" she growls eyeballing Rich Jr.

"Take me outside Verez, I need some fresh air." Casey directs.

Out on the porch, Verez begins pacing before Casey starts to talk. "This kid may be our last chance at Vance. I love your fire Verez, but you have to play this delicately. I'm talking bees with honey kind of thing here Verez," Casey instructs.

"I was thinking more of maggots with plea deals kind of thing," Verez rebuts.

"I've already looked into that. This kid's mom and dad are upstanding citizens, and he's got no record. In fact, it says here that he was checked out on N.C.I.C. for a job as a guard at the federal holding facility. He's clean Verez. We got nothing on him" Casey informs.

"A guard, huh? Yeah, I knew I hated the little weasel," Verez continues to pace the porch.

"Yeah, I considered leaving that info out," Casey confesses.
Verez reaches the end of the porch and turns to go back when the sheriff walks out and closes the door behind him. "I think I got something you might want to hear?" The sheriff announces.

"What now?" she prepares herself for another lump.

"No, this might be good news? It depends on whether or not you think it's worth it, don't know how bad you're wanting this Vance fella'?" the sheriff shrugs.

"You spoke with the devil, and he wants my soul for an air tight case against Vance...give me a knife and I'll sign a contract in blood," she responds half joking.

"What do you have sheriff?" Casey asks from the phone.

"Richie will sign a statement, and says he'll even testify if need be," the sheriff informs them.

"That's what we want to hear, now let's hear what we don't." Verez sits down in one of the rockers.

"He just wants two things, one he says is absolute, but he'd rather have 'em both," the big man eases into it, and Verez can tell it's going to sting. "He wants the dogs back, both of them. The black one, I have had people looking for it, and if Arwood raised it you can bet it's a killer but the Brindle...that's all you guys," the sheriff breaks the news.

"So, I've been demoted to a dog catcher?" Verez asks the phone.

"Looks that way, Verez," Casey responds.

"I've got some good swamp trackers on the other dog's trail, and they shouldn't have too much trouble locating him. A .45 leaves a big hole," the Sheriff shakes his head.

"What if it's dead already? We can't bring it back to life?" Verez asks.

"That's why he said he could understand if the black one couldn't be brought in but the Brindle he wants that one the most," the Sheriff explains. Verez is about to say something when the radio on the Sheriff's side crackles.

"Sheriff Kenny do you read?" the voice calls. The Sheriff unclips his radio.

"Kenny here what do ya' got Bill?" he asks.

"Well, Sheriff, we've been on the dog's trail, and it looks like an eight-foot gator wanted some pit bull for lunch," Bill informs. The Sheriff looks apologetically at Verez.

"Is there enough of our dog left for the boy to identify as his?" the Sheriff asks as Rich Jr. exits the house and listens.

"Well that's the problem Sheriff. We don't know where the dog is," Bill says. The Sheriff and Verez look confused.

"Bill, you just said an eight-foot gator had some pit bull for lunch?"

"I'd say that was the gators plan, but it didn't work out too good for him because the dog is gone and the gator looks like someone run 'em, head first, through a wood chipper." Bill explains.

The Sheriff and Verez look shocked. Rich Jr. beams proudly and nods his head. "What the hell kind of dogs did your uncle make out here?" the Sheriff asks the boy.

"The baddest fighting dogs on earth." Rich Jr. boasts.

"Is the Brindle like the black one?" Verez asks.

"No, no he's ten times bad'er than Black ever was," the boy confesses. Verez and the Sheriff look at one another gravely.

CHAPTER 27

"Did you see the YouTube footage?" Verez asks as she drives. Casey is on the phone's blue tooth connected to the vehicle's radio.

"Yeah, I saw it. I never knew dog fighting was so brutal?" Casey coughs.

"Well that's how the Aztec learned of the dog. That's why they killed Arwood," Verez informs as she scans the landscape looking for Black.

"You really think they came clean across the country to get that dog? They crossed America and killed a man for his dog?" he cannot believe it.

"In their world, a dog is a status symbol and its big money to boot. A dog like that Brindle would definitely be worth killing for," "He was strong enough to mutilate an eight-foot alligator," Verez counters.

"Be careful if you do come across him, Verez. Call for the locals, I mean it, no lone-ranger-crap Verez. It's okay to ask for help when you need it!" Casey lectures.

"I will! If I ever need help, I promise I'll ask boss," Verez concedes partly.

"I want to know something Verez? How did you know about the Aztec tattoo? I mean how'd you know it was them when the boy told you about the tattoo?" Casey questions.

"I am originally from Los Angles and they are one of the gangs in my old neighborhood. They're not real big but they are really violent. Mi Plomo Por Tu Plata is an old Spanish stick up line. It means my lead for your silver. In other words, give me what you got or you're dead!" Verez explains.

"Did you ever see any...

I've got a visual!" Verez cuts him off, as Black hobbles from the bush and goes beneath a bridge ahead of her. She yanks her revolver out after tearing a beef stick out of its pack.

"Where are you at Verez?" Casey asks.

"I'm twelve miles north of Arwood's, just past the old Georgia convenience store. There's a peanut farm. They won't miss my truck," she says, as she shuts the ignition off.

Verez jumps out and runs to the bridge where the dog has disappeared. The revolver in one hand and the meat stick in the other. "Here Black! Hey boy!" Verez calls looking over the edge. She runs to the other side. "Come on Black, here boy! Come on Black!" she calls. Suddenly a swollen head looks up from below the bridge. "That's it, boy! Oh, you're not so bad, huh boy? No, you're a good boy!" Verez coos and is suckered in by the wagging nub of a tail.

She crawls over the guard rail and dangles the meat stick towards the injured animal who hobbles out slowly. There is a concrete slope and holding the guard rail with her gun hand, Verez attempts to lead the dog up the side. "Here boy. Are you hungry honey?" She feels bad for the pathetic creature as it crawls slowly up the ramp towards her, it's left hind leg dragging behind it. Just as it gets within reach of the meat stick, Verez realizes her mistake but not in time.

Black's eyes are those of a lunatic, an emptiness within them causes Verez to catch her breath. As she pulls her arm back, the dog springs upward and bites down on her forearm. Verez's gun arm loops around the guard rail. The dog yanks with his powerful neck muscles causing her to drop the weapon to keep a hold on the metal rail. The revolver rolls, end over end, into the road and as the dog jerks his body again, Verez is nearly ripped from the guard rail. She cries out and with all her strength, holds the rail.

A large tractor-trailer truck roars past and one wheel strikes the revolver sending it skittering near Verez. She looks helplessly at the weapon as she struggles to hold the rail. To go for the gun would mean to fall into the dry creek bed below the bridge with the pit bull, and still she isn't sure that she will be able to grab the gun before she falls. In one mighty jerk, Black makes up her mind, and as he yanks her off the rail, her hand snakes out and plucks the revolver from the road as she falls.

The fall hurts Black as he yelps, for Verez lands on top of him, and the dog's powerful jaws open just long enough for her to roll clear and raise the weapon. She pulls the trigger to find that there is no trigger or hammer. She stares at the primer of the bullet within the cylinder. The huge truck's weight broke the back off the revolver.

Black recovers and slowly crawls towards Verez. She attempts to move back but is against the concrete wall of the bridge. With her injured arm, Verez removes the lock blade from her waist and flips it open. This dog killed an alligator, she thinks as she looks at the small blade of the knife.

Black is nearly upon her when she gets an idea. She points the gun at the crazy beast and begins stabbing the tip of the knife into the primer of the bullet. Over and over she stabs, closer and closer Black crawls until he is on top of her. Ignoring her legs, he intends to go straight for her throat.

She puts the barrel into his mouth. "Say ah!" she growls as the knife point finds the primer and the explosion deafens her beneath the bridge. The slug blows the back of Black's head off and Verez falls back unconscious.

* * *

CHAPTER 28

The blue panel van pulls up to the large garage door of an old brick warehouse. The driver waves at the small camera mounted on the wall of the building. There is a sound of chains banging against the door, and then it begins to slide up and open. The van enters, and the door closes behind it.

Inside the warehouse, men are working on stolen cars with grinders, some stand around watching as the van rolls past.

Diablo exits his office and the van stops "Hurry, show me the dog!" he orders.

The driver gets out and goes to the side of the van and slides the door back. The Brindle stands and turns to Diablo. The gang lord bends down, nearly nose to nose with the pit bull, and stares the dog in the eyes. Panting, the dog's tongue hangs out as it breaths, but when Diablo's eyes lock on to his own, the tongue goes back into his mouth and the panting stops.

The dog does not blink or turn away and the two stare straight into each other's eyes, neither blinking nor looking away. Finally, after nearly a minute, Diablo smiles and stands up. "This dog has no fear! From now on he is Perro del Diablo, the devil's dog!" the gang leader announces, looking around at his men.

He directs his attention to one young Aztec solider. "You Gordo, come here!" Diablo calls to the chubby young thug. "You will take care of Perro del Diablo. Feed, water and exercise him. He is very important to us." Diablo looks around at the men and women who have gathered. "This dog represents us. He's a warrior like us, and he will crush every dog in L.A. The other gangs will see that he is unbeatable. That we are undefeatable, and with this dog our power will spread. We need all the money we can get because we're fightin' Perro del Diablo Friday against Ghost Face's grand champ. He wants to bet fifty grand and when we win, the whole city will know that the Aztecs are making moves," Diablo's speech ends. There are hoots and barks from the soldiers.

Diablo turns to Gordo, "Take Perro del Diablo and chain him to the Sedan's engine we took out this morning. The one on the pallet. Get him some food and water. He is your responsibility Gordo. Don't let me down." Diablo instructs before turning to Flaco, "Come to my office. We need to talk."

Diablo walks into the office, Flaco behind him, and shuts the door. "Can we have the fifty grand by Friday?" Diablo asks, leaning against his desk.

"We have about twenty now. I can collect some outstanding debts, press the Asians at Parkview and move some parts, but fifty thousand dollars...I don't know?" Flaco shakes his head.

"We need this money. I don't want the A.P.G's thinking we're some kind of broke ass crew!" Diablo pounds his fist on the desk.

"Maybe we shouldn't put all our eggs in one basket?" Flaco warns. Diablo dismisses his comment with a wave of a hand.

"Our eggs are safe. This dog cannot..." Diablo is interrupted as Gordo storms into the office.

"Diablo! It's Perro del Diablo! The boy explains.
"I thought I told you to chain him to the engine!" Diablo yells as he and Flaco follow the boy out of the office. Diablo and his general are stunned to discover the dog sauntering across the warehouse floor, dragging the large engine behind him. Perro del Diablo stops to look at them before continuing on his way.

"I did chain him to the engine," the boy says in wonder. Diablo stares in disbelief.

"That's a bad ass dog homie!" Flaco declares.

CHAPTER 29

huck Casey walks through the hall of Ware County Hospital, his eyes scanning the numbers on the doors. His face, a window into his current state, shows the anger that he feels. He told her to ask for help. He told her no Lone Ranger crap. The last four years he has put up with her short fuse and arm sleeve emotions because of how tenacious her work ethic is.

This is it! He draws the line when her cavalier approach to field work nearly costs her life. His anger reaches its height just as he finds her hospital room. He storms in and finds her asleep. He slams the door in an attempt to wake her, but when she does not even flinch he decides to wait for her to come to. He leans against the wall and begins to check his emails on his phone. As he scrolls through the mail his mind goes over all that he wants to say to her when she wakes.

He plans on reminding her about the bank robber that she chased six city blocks until it was only her and the perp. The guy ran into an abandoned warehouse. It ended up being a hand to hand altercation. She wound up with a broken rib and six stitches in her scalp.

He grows more and more upset as he thinks about the half dozen other instances. He gets the "I am woman, hear me roar!" thing, but she is taking it too damn far and he plans to tell her. As he puts his phone back into its case on his belt, a cry escapes Verez's lips. At first, Casey wonders if he should call for a nurse.

"Stop! No Daddy! You're hurting him...stop!" Verez cries out in her sleep.

The sound of Verez whimpering is so alien to Casey that he worries about her condition but stays still.

"No Daddy! Oh, don't die! I will! I'll be strong daddy! I promise I will always be strong, but please daddy don't die! No daddy! Nooo...!"

Verez sits straight up, tears stream down her cheeks and for a moment there is a look in her eyes Casey has never imagined could be. There is a look of helplessness, but it vanishes so quickly that Casey wonders if it ever was there. Verez wipes the tears from her eyes and appears to be embarrassed. Casey turns away and pulls his phone out and answers it.

"Casey here?"

"Yes, I'm in Ware County, but I'll try to get back tonight," He pretends with his back to Verez.

He hopes she takes the time to get herself together. He had read her history and knew about her father being killed in front of her. But she is so damn strong and such a powerful character that he never imagined that her father's death haunted her so much? How could it not? He asked himself, disappointed in his stupidity.

"Alright. Yes, I'll take care of it hon, will do, you too." Casey puts the phone back into his case and turns to face Verez.

She is sitting up, looking at him, with her usual "What's up next boss?" look. He had wanted to tell her off, chew her ass out really good and put her in her place. That's what he wanted to do and he was so damn mad at her for putting her life at risk, but he is just happy to have her back. "Are you okay?" he asks with a softness that shocks even him.

"I'm feeling good. I just have a little scratch, she holds up her casted arm, but you should see the other guy." Verez jokes with not a trace of the tears or anguish Casey had witnessed only moments before.

"You killed our dog, Verez," Casey says attempting to sound upset.

"I had very little choice sir. I considered how much we needed the animal but felt my life would be an unacceptable sacrifice to gain custody of him." She says with a straight face.

From anyone else, Casey would assume that comment to be sarcastic, but from her he wasn't so sure.

"I'm going to contact our Los Angeles office and have them work on getting our dog out there. Blake Marshal is a friend of mine. His office has an active file on your Aztecs and maybe someone on the inside?" he says, gauging her reaction.

"What the hell are you talking about? This is my case! I've put four years of my life into this case...my sweat and my blood..." she holds up the cast, "are in this case and you want to pass it on to another office?" Verez's eyes flash with rage.

Casey realizes quickly that his reaction gauge needn't be too sensitive as Verez, as usual, wears her emotions on her sleeve. "So you think I should send you to Los Angeles to get our dog back? You think you can hold your anger in check and be a team player? Because that's how Blake works out there?" Casey informs.

"I think you should send me. I can't make any promises about the anger thing, but I will promise to try on the team stuff. What I can do is guarantee I will find the dog!" She sits up. Casey looks at her cast and shakes his head.

"Alright, alright Verez, but you'll have to do it without pain killers. The agency has this thing about sending agents out into the field hopped up on narcotics.

"I agree to those terms." She says before looking at her clothes in a chair beside the bed.

Casey follows her eyes and understands; well I'll get out of here and let you get dressed. He starts for the door.

"I want to thank you, Chuck," Verez says warmly. Her voice is soft and completely un-Verez like. Casey turns around.

"It's your case; you should see it to its conclusion." He nods. She shakes her head.

"Not that, the phone call you pretended to take. Thank You!" she smiles sadly. Casey opens the door.

"Don't get mushy on me, Verez. It's strange on you, like watching a crocodile pet a kitten." He smiles before exiting the room.

CHAPTER 30

"Sure, the guy writes a great action scene, but real movies have more content than just sex and explosives Ted." Jacob enters the kitchen, cell phone in its usual position. Sarah sits at the table as Jasmine eats her breakfast. Jacob searches the cupboards for something hastily as if he's in a hurry. "I'll be there in twenty minutes, Ted. Get him to my office because someone has to let him know. Alright, see you in twenty." He hangs up, looks at Sarah, and is about to ask a question when the click of the toaster causes him to look.

"You're a creature of habit, Jacob," she says as he grabs the two pastries, burning his fingers, and tosses them onto a paper towel.

"I'm in a hurry, we're shooting the closing scenes over the next couple of days," Jacob explains, hurrying out of the kitchen.

"You've been in a hurry every morning, for the last four months, it took to shoot the middle scenes and the two months of opening scenes," she says with a sharpness to her tone.

"Well, I have to work honey. It's what keeps us in a million-dollar home in a gated community. We have to make certain sacrifices," he says before exiting the kitchen. As Sarah hears the door close she turns to Jasmine.

"Our family shouldn't be one of them. He used to at least kiss us goodbye, huh," Sarah brushes her hand over Jasmine's head.

The little girl continues to eat as if she has heard nothing. Sarah watches her daughter eat the toaster pastry. She thinks about how much the child depends on her and how Jacob has begun to move further and further away from them. If he isn't at the studio, he's in his home office until all hours of the night. As Jacob has drifted further away, Sarah has felt herself move closer and closer to her daughter.

She can't decide if it's her way of making up for Jacob not being a bigger part of the child's life or if it's because he seems to have become a smaller part of her own? Either way, she decides, something is happening to the three of them, and she feels powerless to stop it.

Sarah jumps up, as a thought enters her head, and begins cleaning up around the kitchen in an attempt to take her mind off what she is thinking.

It's not the first time it has crossed her mind...it's as if she may, one day, be forced to choose between Jacob and Jasmine. It's as if he's spending so much time apart from them because of Jasmine's condition and he seems to be uncomfortable around his child. She hates to think that the man she has loved for so long, the father of her child, could be such a selfish person. If she were forced to make a choice, she thinks looking at Jasmine lick her little fingers, then it would not even be a close decision.

Sarah is immediately overcome with guilt for even thinking such thoughts. "What happened to us?" she whispers. "We need something," she prays silently, "something to save us before it's too late."

CHAPTER 31

Verez enters the conference room to find two other agents sitting at the long table, huge tinted windows allow for the Los Angeles cityscape to be viewed without the discomfort of the California sun's sweltering heat. On the table, a projection machine sits next to folders filled with paperwork. The older man stands first as she enters followed by the other man.

"Dominica Verez. I'm Blake Marshall and this," Blake motions toward the other man, "is Rogers Hess. Rogers's over our S.T.G., Security Threat Group division." Blake and Rogers shake her hand before Blake offers her a seat, which she accepts.

"Now I understand that there was a murder of a possible informant, but it had nothing to do with the victim's having been a witness, and the murder's not the primary reason for why you are here but rather to find and return a dog to a witness? Can you help me understand why the dog takes precedence over a murder?" Blake is baffled.

Verez explains the entire situation, from Vance's Atlanta Empire and the death of multiple witnesses to Ron Arwood and Vance's business dealing. She concludes with the dog's YouTube footage and the coincidental murder of Arwood followed by Rich Jr.'s deal to testify.

When she has concluded her story, Blake sits back and whistles. "Ol' Chuck has a real cluster fuck going on out there in Atlanta." I'm not entirely surprised to hear the Aztecs are involved though. Ever since one of their original founders was released from Pelican Bay, three years ago, they've been rising in the ranks of L.A.'s more active gangs." Blake turns the light off and the projector on.

On the screen is a man in his late fifties, Verez guesses. His hair is past his shoulders and so black it's blue where it's not gray. He has a weathered look, and his shirt is open revealing a large tattoo of a senorita in a sombrero on his chest. He is short but stocky and there is a look in his eyes. A look of a dangerous man and Verez shivers as a chill goes up her spine.

"His name is Danny Rejas, AKA Diablo, and this guy is as ruthless and ambitious as any I've ever heard of. Since his release, Blake flips through several slides, each showing dead bodies on the streets – the other founding members have all met violent ends." Blake lets the next picture remain on the screen.

"That's their headquarters now. It's like a fortress, and since they are such a tight knit neighborhood gang, it's been impossible to infiltrate them and get a guy inside," Rogers explains.

"Diablo's office is in there, and we know they are involved with a chop shop, drug trafficking and as you've said, dog fighting. The problem is what we know can't get us a search warrant because we have nobody inside to give us the evidence we need to present for an affidavit," Blake elaborates.

"That's because we can't get a guy inside," Rogers repeats.

"Well, maybe, it's not a guy but a gal you fella's are needing?" Verez smiles.

"That might not be such a bad idea? If we could get you in, you could look around, and if you saw anything illegal happening, you could swear to it and that would be enough to get us a search warrant," Blake appears to think on the matter.

"I need this dog. I understand that you guys want to shut them down but if I don't get a visual on the dog and you send the team in the dog might be being held somewhere else and they could kill it to destroy evidence of a murder? I don't mind the team thing, but let's remember we all have stakes in this thing," Verez warns.

"Oh, no, absolutely, and if you are able to get inside it's your show all we want is enough to get a warrant and won't make a move until you feel sure we can get your dog," Blake assures her.

"Your timeline puts the dog here what...three weeks ago?" Rogers asks.

"It will be three weeks tomorrow, why?" Verez asks."

"Well, every Friday the Aztecs, supposedly, have dog fighting matches in their warehouse. How do you know that your dog hasn't lost and isn't laying under a sofa at the city dump by now?" Rogers asks.

Verez looks at the two men for a moment. You haven't seen the YouTube footage of this dog's fight, have you?" she asks, before removing the tablet from her briefcase. As the footage ends, both men sit back in their seats.

"Well, as soon as you get a visual on the dog, and report it to us, we can secure a warrant. The dog's the priority, but be on the lookout for any other possible activity.

Chopped cars, drugs, guns, dog fighting or even a mattress with the tags ripped off. I want all you can collect Verez," Blake looks at the paused footage.

"Yeah, Diablo would have killed his mother for a dog like that. There's no telling what kind of money they'll make off of that monster?" Blake hands Verez a stack of folders. "Familiarize yourself with these characters. They're all regulars at the Friday night fights the Aztec host. Me and Rogers will get the D.A. to get a court order to get you inside the place, but after that the rest is up to you," he explains. Verez puts the folder in the case along with the tablet.

"I've worked undercover before." she informs.

As they get up, Blake turns to her. "You're familiar with this area of Los Angeles, aren't you?"

"Yes, I was raised in Los Angeles," she smiles, "Oh yeah, where about?" Rogers asks, getting the door for her.

"East L.A.," she says as she walks out and both Blake and Rogers look at one another in surprise.

An hour later Verez is driving the rental through an area of her old neighborhood and sees Aztec graffiti on the sides of stone walls and vacant houses she finds herself on the street she grew up on and slowly drives until she stops in front of the home with a chain link fence enclosing the front yard. The street light above her is still burnt out. She thinks, just as it was that night twenty years earlier

Then the memory comes back, and she sees herself as a child standing at the gate screaming for the men to stop kicking her father. She sees the dark man get out of the sedan and watches as he lights the cigarette. The flame sends shadows dancing across his features but still, she cannot recognize him before he exhales smoke from his nostrils, like a dragon, extinguishing the lighter's flame then he shoots her father.

She begins crying. "No Daddy! Please don't die!" the child cries.

"Be strong." Always be strong. He tells the child.

"I'm trying dad. I'm trying," Verez sobs as she wipes the tears from her eyes.

* * *

CHAPTER 32

The warehouse is loud with the talking of hundreds of people. Bleachers have been set up around the circular pit and the set up looks like a model of the Roman Coliseum, but many of the people are standing about rather than sitting in their seats. Several different gangs, and people from all over the county are in attendance. Even a group of white kids from Malibu are here doing their best gangster impressions. The noise is deafening, and Diablo stands in the midst of it all, anxious to show them all what his titan is capable of.

Smoke from tobacco and marijuana rises to the lights above, which are the only ones on in the warehouse, and the smoke has caused the whole area to appear illuminated by a magic fog. From the dark, Ghost face and several of his soldiers appear. Ghost Face is the leader of the largest neighborhood gang in the area. The A.P.G.'s or Alton Park Gangsters, and that makes him the most powerful man around. Ghost Face gives Diablo a head nod, a sign of respect and greetings, Diablo returns the gesture. One of Ghost Face's men walks Keeta, the A.P.G.'s grand champ.

"Where is the dog you are wanting to lose fifty grand with?" Ghost Face leans close to Diablo and yells over the crowd.

"He's on his way. Keeta's looking very good!" Diablo yells back, pretending to look the blonde pit bull over.

"Yeah, he does, and he'll look real good eating steak tonight after he wins me fifty thousand of your dollars and kills your dog!" Ghost Face yells back smugly.

Diablo only nods. Suddenly there is silence from one corner of the crowd. People part the way as Gordo and Flaco, led by Perro del Diablo, walk toward the pit. The noise subsides as everyone stares down at the new dog.

"Where the hell did you get that thing?" Ghost Face asks.

Diablo knows the dog is a sight to behold, only about twenty inches tall but over two feet thick and as solid as an anvil with legs. A two-inch-thick callous wraps completely around the dog's neck from years of having a chain around it, and his ears are cropped so low they hardly exist.

"His name is Perro del Diablo and tonight he eats Keeta," Diablo informs the A.P.G. leader.

Ghost Face loses his famous confidence before he walks to the other side of the pit, where Keeta is being held. The people are taking their seats, and the noise has risen once again to ear bleeding levels. Directly across from one another, each dog is held by its chain. Keeta's back paws stand at the edge of the pit, its front paws dangle in the air as its chain holds it back. Perro del Diablo stands calmly looking at his opponent. He looks back into the eyes of the blonde dog and sees the animal is crazy with blood lust and knows that if given the opportunity it will kill him and so he decides Keeta will have no such opportunity.

The noise is numbing but he hears only the sound of his beating heart, which grows steadier. Perro del Diablo waits for the slightest release of his collar, he waits for the slightest release. When it happens, the collar is broken and in one motion he leaps across the pit, bites down on the unsuspecting throat of Keeta, and drops to his hind feet. Using the years of balance training, he stands up right and begins whipping the body of Keeta, back and forth from side to side, until a loud pop is heard that silences the entire audience.

In a room that, only seconds earlier, was as loud as any rock concert, the sound of a cherry from a burning cigarette can be heard fizzling before a single voice interrupts the mass silence.

"That's a bad ass dog homes," Flaco declares.

In half an hour, while the crowd is still leaving, Diablo is at his desk counting the fifty thousand. It took less than five seconds to win. There is a knock at the office door. "Come in!" Diablo yells, not looking up as he counts. The door opens and Flaco enters with two white guys.

"Someone wants to talk with you Diablo," Flaco says shutting the door.

Diablo continues to count for a moment longer before stopping to look up at the white guys.

"What do you want?" he asks impatiently. One of the white guys steps up to the desk.

"I want to fight your dog," the kid says arrogantly.

"He'll kick your ass," Diablo laughs.

"No, not me, my dog. I have a dog I want to fight with yours." The kid isn't smiling. Diablo's smile slowly fades.

"I'm not doing this for fun boy. It's expensive, you'll have to pay to play. What do you want to put up?" Diablo looks the kid over.

"I'll put twenty up," the kid says quickly enough that Diablo can tell the rich kid can come up with more.

"Tonight, we put up fifty large each...I don't pull Perro del Diablo out for nothing less than seventy-five," Diablo tests the waters willing to drop to fifty if he has to. The kid seems to be thinking before he looks Diablo in the eyes and nods his head. Got 'em! Diablo thinks to himself.

"Okay, it will take me a few weeks, but I'll have it," the kid agrees.

"That may be good for you because I'll be fighting Perro del Diablo every Friday night...who knows he might lose a leg and give your dog half a chance?" Diablo laughs.

The kid leaves the office. Flaco turns to Diablo after he shuts the door. "You think they're serious?" he asks sitting on the couch.

"I think those rich kids would do anything to look like gangsters. They just don't know what all comes with it." Diablo smiles.

"Are you serious about fighting Perro del Diablo every Friday night? That's a lot of fighting for one dog, bro?" Flaco asks,

"Diablo smiles before repeating Flaco's line. "That's a bad ass dog homes."

CHAPTER 33

"**W**hat do you mean...are you saying that four hundred dollars a week isn't enough for taking care of Perro del Diablo?" Diablo asks, looking around the office at Flaco and Fan, the leader of the Asian connection boys, who sits on the couch.

"No, that's not what I'm saying Diablo. I'm saying other brothers are making a thousand dollars or better a week selling, stealing cars and stuff like that. I only make four hundred and my dad's in prison, my mom works two jobs and I have six brothers and sisters." Gordo pleads.

Diablo sits silent for a moment before turning and opening his safe. Stacks of bills fill the metal box and Diablo removes one. He turns to Gordo and peels five one hundred dollar bills from the stack. "I will raise your pay a hundred dollars more each week. He starts to hand Gordo the money but pulls it back. "I want you to take extra good care of Perro del Diablo, Gordo," he hands the cash to the still obviously unhappy kid. "Do not become greedy little brother...it's a very ugly thing, greed. Now go clean up Perro del Diablo's area and make sure he has food and water." Diablo dismisses the boy who walks out still unsatisfied.

"Now Fan, you wanted to talk to me about something?" Diablo waves the Asian gang leader over. Fan stands and walks to the chair in front of Diablo's desk and sits.

"I wanted to speak to you about the Parkview apartments and a business proposition," Fan explains.

Diablo's eyes squint. "What kind of proposition?"

"Well, Fan continues, Parkview is Asian territory and we want an equal share of the profits that come out of the apartments. It's only fair that we get an equal..." Fan elaborates before Diablo holds a hand up and the Asian stops talking.

"Equality is a plea used by the weak begging the strong to give them what they have not earned. Let me tell you a tale of equality Fan. One day the rabbit king goes before the council of the beasts. On the council there sits the lion, the tiger, the bear and the wolf. The rabbit king stands and demands equality for rabbits. The council speaks in private before the lion turns and asks one simple question...but rabbit, where are your claws? There are eleven members in the A.C.B. Fan and most are just children.".

"But Diablo, all I'm..." A knock at the door interrupts Fan, and he appears frustrated.

"Come in!" Diablo yells. The door opens, and it is one of the Aztec females.

"There's two white boys here with a dog and a bag of cash? They said you would know what time it is?" Rachel says chewing gum. Diablo smiles and looks at Fan.

"Come on, Rabbit, let me show you why there is no equality among men or beast."

Diablo stands and walks out of the office followed by Fan and Flaco. The two rich kids from Malibu stand with a pit bull between them, the taller one holding the dog's leather leash and the other holding a duffle bag of cash. Diablo greets them.

"What's up gangsters? I didn't think you two were going to come back."

"We just had to get our paper right bro...seventy five grand right?" the tall one asks, all business.

Diablo looks down at the dog. It's a nice-looking animal, but not half Perro del Diablo's weight and the dog is completely without scars.

"I don't get it? Does it know karate or something?" Diablo ask the two boys.

"We figure our dog has as good a shot at winning as yours does...they're both pit bulls." the tall one reasons.

"How many fights has your red pit won?" Diablo asks while he waves Gordo over.

"Two, he's only fought twice but won both of 'em," the tall one brags.

"Get Perro del Diablo ready for war," he instructs Gordo who walks towards the back.

"What kind of dogs did he fight?" Diablo asks, winking at Flaco.

"It was the same dog," the taller one starts to say before the short one speaks and Diablo realizes that one is stupid and the other is handicapped.

"Yeah, he fought mom's Speck and whooped him good. Didn't he Steve?" the handicapped one says excitedly, Flaco turns away in shame.
"Shut up Greg! Yeah, he fought the same dog, it's a German Shepherd," Steve, the stupid one, says.

"How old are you two?" Diablo asks the two brothers.

"I'm eighteen and Steve's seventeen...I'm the older brother!" Greg says proudly.

Flaco motions for Diablo, and they walk a few feet away.

"These are just some dumb kids bro, the one's not even right in the head, get 'em out of here so we can get back to work," He says hoping to spare the two.
"They ain't leaving with that money. Stupid people's money is as good as anybody else's...I thought better of you Flaco, how dare you discriminate against those less intelligent than yourself! I'm ashamed of you bro," Diablo laughs as he turns back to the two brothers.

"Let's go see which one of us is going to be rich and who's gonna be pissed? I can't wait to see which one of our dogs is going to win!" Diablo feigns wonder as they all move to the pits where Perro del Diablo is waiting, at the end of a chain, on the edge of the pit.
The red pit bull sees Perro del Diablo and stops a few feet from the pit. The red animal's smell says it all. Perro del Diablo catches the fear in the animal's scent.

"Get up there stupid!" stupid Steve, the taller boy says as he pulls the red dog to the edge of the pit by the thick leather leash.

"Give the bag to Rachel to hold until it's over," Diablo instructs as Rachel reaches for the bag."

"Where's your seventy five?" Steve asks suspiciously.

Diablo smiles and turns to Flaco, "Would you go to the safe and grab seventy five out and bring it?" Diablo asks calmly.

Flaco does not wish to see the scared dog being slaughtered and quickly walks to the office. Gordo drops Perro del Diablo into the pit and Steve attempts to get the red dog into the hole in the floor where Perro del Diablo waits. Fan looks around at the few Aztec standing around. The soldiers not laughing look ashamed.

"He doesn't want to fight Steve! Maybe we shouldn't, that other dog looks real mean!" Greg warns.

"Shut up Greg! A bet's a bet!" he says looking at Diablo who struggles not to laugh.

"A bet is a bet!" Diablo agrees.

Finally, Steve pushes the dog into the pit and Perro del Diablo starts towards him when the red dog yelps in fear and turns away, Perro del Diablo stops. Flaco arrives with the money and sees the two dogs in the pit, Perro del Diablo looking around at the people above and the other animal with its head against the pit wall in fear.

"Well boy, it looks like your dog won't fight," Diablo says with a sad smile on his face.

"Can we get the money back?" stupid Steve asks.

Diablo shakes his head slowly. "A bet is a bet."

Steve wraps the thick leash around his hand twice before leaning down and strapping the red dog. "Fight you stupid coward! Fight!" he whips the terrified animal.

Diablo and a few others laugh. Flaco turns away. Steve whips the yelping dog over and over as his brother tries to stop him, Perro del Diablo jumps up and grabs the leash in his powerful jaws and with a jerk of his neck, yanks Steve down into the pit.

The boy lands on his hands and knees and immediately backs up against the wall. Perro del Diablo growls loud not intending to hurt the human, only to get him to stop hitting the dog but as Perro del Diablo stands there growling, the red dog jumps in between he and Steve. There is another scent over the fear. The red dog is willing to fight and die in defense of the human that moments earlier, was whipping him.

Confused but prepared, Perro del Diablo starts to attack when the other boy drops down and scoops the red dog up in his arms and kicks at Perro del Diablo who backs up instantly.

"I'm the big brother! Let's go home, Steve! We're not fighting Red no more!" Greg says as he, Steve and Red get out of the pit.

Diablo turns to Fan. "Just when you think you've seen it all?" Diablo laughs.

"Can we get back to our conversation?" Fan asks as Diablo collects the money from Rachel.

"What conversation?" the gang lord asks.

"What we were talking about..." Fan reminds him.

"Oh, equality, right? It's not gonna happen." Diablo walks off. "But you didn't even..." Fan tries to speak but Diablo cuts him off.

"Go Rabbit, before I have rabbit stew!" Diablo yells over his shoulder entering his office.

Moments later Fan gets into a car. His brother Tom, waits behind the wheel. "He laughed at us." I knew he would," Tom says starting the car.

"Yeah, but what'll make him laugh will make 'em cry!" Fan says as he watches Gordo walk the Brindle pit bull around the back fenced in area across from where they are parked.

CHAPTER 34

The sun is setting behind the sky scape of   Los Angeles casting calico shadows across the city. Gordo walks, head down, alone and deep in thought. So deep in thought, that he doesn't notice the red Civic, with tinted windows, that drives up to slowly move beside him as he walks. The passenger side window rolls down and Fan peers out at the chubby teen.

"Hey kid!" Fan calls.

"What are you doing here? This is Aztec territory!" Gordo looks around nervously.

"Relax kid. I got some business to talk to you about." As the car slows to a stop and the back door opens.

"What kind of business? Gordo asks, before stooping and looking suspiciously at Fan.

"Twenty thousand dollars' worth of business, be the easiest money you ever make kid," Fan smiles.

Gordo appears suspicious and looks around to find the industrial area void of any other people. He squints his eyes at Fan who motions toward the open rear door of the car with a head nod. Gordo takes a deep breath and gets into the car before Fan, smiling, rolls the window up and the Civic drives away.

A block away, Perro del Diablo lays beneath the work bench he is chained to within the warehouse. He attempts to work out the day's events in his head but cannot grasp all that has happened. He smelled the fear on the red dog, as strong as he had ever smelled it on any animal, but instantly it changed to the scent of one fully willing to die.   He could not understand how a dog could change immediately? To be afraid for its own survival one moment but then willing to die for a human the next.

The human was hurting the dog but that made no difference to the animal? The fear was not gone; the smell did not quite change, but rather became so much stronger that it seemed to be a different scent. The red dog, Perro del Diablo decides, was more afraid to lose the human than it was to lose its own life? Afraid for another? How could that be possible? He does not know, as fear is alien to him but fear of another's life being lost is incomprehensible.

The warehouse has grown but a noise gets his attention. Someone is coming to the back where he lays beneath the bench. He recognizes the scent and is surprised to find it alone without that of the other. The one that smells of sharp rottenness. This one smells of the wind that comes after the rain in the swamp and he is coming to the work bench. Flaco walks to the bench and sits on a large spool of cable wire in the corner. For a long time, he and Perro del Diablo look at one another.

"You are special, not like other dogs. There is something very different about you my friend." Flaco breaks the silence. "I saw you spare the dog. I saw you defended the dog," Flaco shakes his head. "Dog's don't do that. Not fighting dogs." Flaco smiles at the dog beneath the bench. "When I was a boy I used to think that when we die we came back as animals. That the best people could return as dogs or dolphins...creatures that make the world a better place. That's crazy isn't it?" Flaco shakes his head.

Perro del Diablo does not understand Flaco's words but he understands his meaning. He understands that he does not ever have to worry about being hit by this man. That a strange warmness comes over him when this human is near and that the man's smell is a good one.

"You and me, we are a lot alike my friend. Life has happened to us. We were born in worlds that we really do not belong to, but we've had to do what we've had to do to survive. Perhaps one day," Flaco stands to leave, "we will find a world where we belong?"

Flaco smiles and nods to the dog before he walks away but the warm feeling and the scent stays with Perro de Diablo long into the night.

CHAPTER 35

There is a long line outside of the warehouse, as men and women slowly file into the brick building, an attractive Latino woman walks up to a large Hispanic man with gold teeth and stands beside him in line. He looks at her flashing his golden smile. She smiles back, and he takes a hold of her cast as they enter the building together.

The security sees the man and gives her the look they give all sexy senoritas before letting them pass into the interior of the building. Inside, Verez is surprised by the number of people and the level of noise. She looks around and sees nothing but darkness, as the only lights on are those above the bleachers and the pit. From the darkness come the sounds of dogs barking. She thinks. The crowd is so loud that she cannot be sure.

Behind the closed-door of his office, Diablo is not bothered by the noise from the crowd but rather what Flaco has told him.

"Why the hell won't Perro del Diablo be fighting tonight?" Diablo demands, walking from around his desk to stand in front of Flaco.

"Because two hours ago Bullet's place was raided by the Feds. They confiscated everything, including the dog. They charged Bullet for killing a whole car full of Northsiders." Flaco informs Diablo who is livid.

"What about any of the dogs fighting tonight? Can we get someone to let us fight instead?" He asks desperately.

"No. I tried that already. Nobody wants their dog to fight Perro del Diablo, not after the Santa Cruz' boys brought that hyena they stole from the zoo," Flaco says, and Diablo looks down at the hyena skin rug he is standing on. "Cowards." Diablo growls.

"That's the trouble with having an unbeatable dog. People learn their dogs can't beat it...nobody wants to give money away or watch their dog die," Flaco continues.

"So, what, there are no more fights for him?" Diablo looks as if he's close to snapping.

Flaco recognizes the look. "No, I'm sure I can get us something; Oakland, San Fran or somewhere? There's always someone who thinks they have the baddest dog around,"

Diablo walks to the door before turning back to Flaco. "If we don't find other fights he's no good to us Flaco," he says before exiting the office.

Flaco understands what that means and shakes his head because he knows that Diablo will kill Perro del Diablo rather than let another gang have a chance at getting him. Keeping the animal when it cannot be fought would never occur to the gang lord because in his world if it made no profit, it made no sense. Flaco knows he must find a challenger because he cannot bear for the dog to die as so many have in the past. The crowd roars. Flaco snaps out of his reverie and walks out into the noise of the warehouse.

When Diablo reaches the bleachers, he sees Verez and smiles at her. The smile causes a shiver to run down her spine, but she returns it because she knows who he is and if she is going to get what she needs it will come easier from the top than from some soldier. He makes his way over to where she sits and takes the seat beside her.

"You are definitely not from around here; I would not forget a woman as beautiful as you!" Diablo yells over the noise.

"I'm on medical leave," she informs him, showing off her cast. "Where are you from originally?" Diablo looks her body over. She can almost feel his eyes physically skimming over her body. His voice makes her shiver.

"San Antonio, I came to visit some old friends, and I met him." she motions to the man with the gold teeth who smiles from a few seats away.

"Gold mouth? What's the finest woman in East L.A. doing with the fattest tub?" he asks.

"He said there was a dog fighting tonight that was unbeatable," she cuts to the chase and sees the nickel-plated revolver in his waist.

"Perro del Diablo, It is true he cannot be beaten, but tonight he will not fight.

There will be several fights tonight, but he will not fight until next week," he informs her.

Diablo follows her eyes to the gun in his waist. He removes it and holds it proudly! "I call it reaper, for the souls it has taken," he hands the gun to her. Verez looks it over as if she's never held a gun before. She runs her fingers across six notches cut in the side of the barrel. "For the six souls it's taken." He turns the gun over in her hand. "The serial number is my birth date and six, six, six...it's why I am called Diablo. This gun is the only thing my father ever gave me. It was a present for my fourteenth birthday." He explains as she hands the gun back to him.

"Will Perro del Diablo be fighting next week for sure?" she asks in her best feminine voice.

"Yes, that is if you will be here to watch him?" Diablo flirts.

"I'm on two weeks medical leave. That's perfect," she smiles.

"What happened and what is your job in San Antonio?" he asks with his hand on her knee.

"I was bitten by a dog. I'm a dog catcher," she smiles. "Then you should enjoy this!" he laughs but she does not.

She watches the brutal fights as dog after dog is taken out of the pit, bloodied, dying or dead and fights the urge to stop it, to call in the cavalry and end it now, but to do that would jeopardize the investigation. And so Verez watches the animals being abused and when the crowd all begins to leave, she blends in and exits the warehouse as Diablo searches the faces of those making their way out. She does not know why but she hates the man. Not as an officer of the law hates the lawless but something more. A hatred that comes from her stomach and she cannot wait to put him away. Vance she wants, but Diablo she needs to take down.

* * *

CHAPTER 36

"It's completely understandable to feel that way Verez. The guy's a scary bastard. We can get a search warrant on the dog fighting alone, but we have no idea if the entire gang will be there or if the dog is being held in another location. We raid the joint and half the other Aztecs are out. Well, they'll get hip to the heat and any evidence that can be destroyed will be." Blake chews on the end of a pen.

"Not to mention, those that hide. It's hell searching for a suspected gang member who's in the wind in the gang's neighborhood. Every damn house within their territory is subject to hide 'em and they know every face and vehicle that does and doesn't belong," Rogers chimes in.

"If you are not comfortable with going back then we'll use what we have and get a search warrant. It's up to you Verez," Blake plays the guilt game.

"No, the guy gives me the creeps. That's all. A search warrant won't do it. We need a surprise raid as well and the next time I'm going in wired. Once I have a visual on the dog, I'll give the word and in comes the team. I'm completely comfortable; whatever gets this creep behind bars and that dog in my custody." Verez looks at the pyramid on the wall showing the rank of the Aztec's within the gang. "The one who calls himself Diablo is at the top. His eyes are black and soulless."

"Diablo, he certainly is the Devil," she thinks "And L.A., no the world will be better with him off the streets." The cold chill comes again but she ignores it.

Blake and Rogers are talking tactical entrance scenarios. Blake looks up at her. "The best way is through the front while they're all gathered around the pit. You good with that?" he asks.

Verez nods her head and smiles, "Yeah I'll be surrounded by the most dangerous gangsters in Los Angeles when the FBI busts in and catches them all in the act of a federal crime. What could go wrong in that situation?" she thinks, but the smile does not betray her apprehension.

"Great," Blake says, "we're all set then."

CHAPTER 37

D iablo sits in his chair, Rachel sits upon the desk, and his hand rests upon her leg. His hand begins to slide up her thigh when there is a knock at the door. Diablo looks frustrated. "Come back in half an hour!" he yells at the knocker.

"I think you're going to want to come out for this, Diablo," comes the muffled response from Flaco on the other side of the closed door.

"Come in Flaco!" Diablo barks. The door opens and Flaco steps half in.

"Fan's here," he says and Diablo appears ready to explode. "You interrupt me for Fan!" he nearly screams.

"He's with Ghost Face," Flaco explains. Diablo screws his face in surprise.

In the back of the warehouse, Perro del Diablo eats a bowl of ground beef that Gordo has just prepared. As the dog hungrily devours the bowl's contents, the boy rolls up a small baggy with a white powdery substance within it and stuffs the baggy into his pocket.

In the front area of the warehouse at that exact moment, Diablo walks out to find Fan and Ghost Face waiting. "What's up, Ghost Face, did you adopt an Asian?" Diablo laughs. Ghost Face chuckles as well, but Fan is all business.

"I'm here to make a bet." The Asian gang leader does not smile. "What's the bet, Rabbit?" Diablo gets serious.

"My dog against yours, right here and now. My two hundred and fifty thousand against your claim to Parkview apartments," Fan challenges.

"First, I make over a million a year out of those apartments and second, where the hell did you get two hundred and fifty grand?" he asks the Asian gangster. Fan opens the duffle bag and shows him the money. Diablo looks at Ghost Face.

"You backin' this rabbit?" he asks.

"He made me an offer I couldn't refuse." The A.P.G. smiles.

"Perro del Diablo has a fight tonight Diablo..." Flaco attempts to explain.

"Tell Gordo to prepare him for war!" Diablo growls looking at Fan.

Tom walks a Rottweiler into the warehouse and Diablo smiles. "Rabbits exist only to be food for other animals. At least you could have gotten a fighting dog Rabbit. Do I have a sign out front welcoming idiots with money or something?" Diablo laughs.

As the group makes their way to the pit Perro del Diablo is brought by Gordo. From their point of view, all appears as it should because Perro del Diablo's view is very different. The group appears to have melted into one colorless blob and their voices are distorted and monstrous sounding.

At the pit the Rottweiler tries to leap across to where the Brindle colored foe stands but the chain keeps him on his own side. Diablo gives the signal and with his collar broke, Perro del Diablo collapses forward into the pit where the Rottweiler attacks. Perro del Diablo raises, lifting the Rottweiler up as well, but is unable to balance himself and collapse back to the pit floor where the large opponent continues to attack. Fan's dog is doing no real harm as his teeth bite down on the two-inch calloused area around Perro del Diablo's neck but it's clear that Diablo's dog has lost. "Get up! Get up, you worthless piece of shit! Diablo rages from above. After another minute, even the Rottweiler is exhausted.

"It's over Diablo!" Ghost Face explains.

"No! It's not over!"

Diablo walks to the work bench as Ghost Face drops into the pit and pulls Fan's dog off of Perro del Diablo who lays in a daze upon the floor of the pit. Fan starts to say something to Diablo, who walks back with a roll of duct tape in his hands, when Ghost Face pulls him away. Diablo drops down into the hole, where the dog has still not risen to his feet and begins taping the dog's back paws together. Flaco starts to say something but thinks better of it and turns away gritting his teeth.

After he has secured the animal's front paws together with the tape, Diablo pulls the dog out of the pit and drags the bound animal through the back door. Outside, Diablo walks his burden to a large horse trough full of black water. Diablo heaves the dog up and dumps it into the muck, holding the taped paws, Diablo growls as he watches the bubbles rise and feels the animal's legs kick, hopelessly in a panic. When the bubbles have finally stopped, and the legs cease to kick, the gang lord's rage is still not satisfied.

Diablo pulls the lifeless body of Perro del Diablo completely out of the trough and with a mighty effort, swings the dog's body high into the air, like he's swinging an ax, and slams the body upon its side, violently to the ground. Diablo spits on the dog and storms back into the warehouse, slamming the door shut. The animal lays still and silent, somewhere a car horn honks and a helicopter can be heard off in the distance but other than that here is no noise to disturb the silence.

Suddenly the animal coughs and the remaining water, which was not expelled from his lungs when Diablo slammed him to the ground, and unwittingly performed the first and most important step of resuscitating a drowning victim, is ejected from his throat and lungs. At first, he only whines in agony. His lungs burn, and his head aches unbearably. He does not understand why the world spins and he is unable to rise, but slowly things grow still, and he realizes his paws are bound.

He shifts his legs and, thanks to the oily water, can free a front paw. It takes several minutes but he is able to get a rear paw loose the same way and slowly stands. He is unsteadied but begins walking the edge of the fence and finds an opening between a gateway secured by a loose chain. The space is just barely wide enough for him to squeeze through and out into the city streets.

The afternoon sun burns hot, and his fur is dry by the time he reaches the interstate. The hours slip away as he stumbles, in a daze, along back roads, train tracks and finally through a golf course to a fence line. He follows the wooden fence until he reaches an area that has been destroyed by a fallen tree branch.

The exhausted dog clamors over the wreckage into a quiet backyard. There is a child's playhouse which he enters. He collapses to the grass floor and is immediately overcome by sleep. Drugged, beaten, drowned and slammed into revivification before walking hours beneath the California sun, he cannot put this day behind him soon enough.

While he is dropping into the deepest sleep he has ever known Flaco is cleaning up the area of the warehouse that Perro del Diablo has called home for the past two and a half months.

The Aztec General is secretly grieving the dog's death but hiding it well as he reaches for the dog's bowl.

Rising, bowl in hand, he notices a powdery substance on the bowl's rim.
Running his finger over it, he collects a small amount and touches it to his tongue.

The acrid taste is mediciny and instantly he figures out what has occurred.

Ten minutes later Flaco and Diablo stand near the spot where Perro Del Diablo's body should have still been.

Looking down at the pieces of duct tape and the dried mud puddle Diablo is awe struck.

"The damn thing is still alive!" Diablo says.

To which Flaco simply states, "That's a bad ass dog homes."

Diablo growls as he walks back into the warehouse, leaving Flaco alone.

The Aztec General stares out at the city below the setting sun.

"Go find the world that You belong in my friend." Flaco says out loud with a smile before turning to return to the world he must remain in.

CHAPTER 38

Ten hours later the warehouse is packed with the largest crowd that ever attended the fights and, for some reason, the security is tighter than it was the last time she came. The cell phone in her hand is actually the wire and so she is free to wear a rather revealing and tight halter top with spandex Capri style pants.

"It will take suspicion off of you," Blake had said when she came out of the dressing room.

"Yeah, everyone will be too busy drooling to ever suspect you're an undercover agent...hell they might be in handcuffs by the time they realize that you've got 'em under arrest," Rogers jokes.

She feels naked and every man in the building seems to be staring at her. A guy with a cane, not because he needs it but as part of his attire, scoots closer to her until only the width of his cane separates them. She can't wait until she gets a visual on the dog and gives the awaiting team the word. She feels like a piece of meat in the midst of a pack of wolves.

What is taking so long? Something is wrong, she thinks, as she hears others growing restless. Just when a few people begin to yell about the holdup, Diablo makes his way through the crowd before dropping down into the pit and signaling for everyone to quiet down. It takes a few seconds, but slowly the crowd grows quieter until the Aztec leader speaks.

"My brothers and sisters, friends and associates...I regret to tell you that Perro del Diablo will not be fighting tonight..." the crowd boos and growls and Diablo smiles patiently waiting for them to quiet down so he can continue. Verez feels a sickening feeling as the gang leader motions them all to quiet down again. They will have to rely on the search warrant alone, she thinks, just before he continues.

"The reason is because of a betrayer, a snake in my own family," Diablo signals to someone in the darkness beyond the lights. A young tattooed teen brings another heavy set young man, whose hands are bound behind his back, out and shoves him into the pit. The bound boy's face is battered, bleeding and swollen.

"There is one thing that calls for no other punishment than death...disloyalty. Disloyalty is a disease and is contagious if not cured swiftly," Diablo places a cigarette in his mouth before two jets of smoke extinguish the lighter's flame, Verez's flashback comes and she can now see the features of the dark man who killed her father all those years ago. It's him.

Her heart races as he removes Reaper, his revolver, she looks around for a weapon and sees the cane beside her. There are two rows of people on the bleacher seats between her row and the pit where Diablo is lowering the gun to Gordo's head. Verez leaps the two rows.

"FBI! Drop your weapon!" she screams as she slams the cane down on the gang's leader's hand. Sending the weapon to the pit floor. Verez is caught with a body blow from Diablo that takes the wind out of her and sends her back against the pit's concrete edge.

Diablo kicks Gordo out of the way and grabs Verez by her hair intending to knee her in the face. As his knee raises she turns her head while at the same time raising his knee higher with her left arm. The momentum takes the man off his feet and slams the back of his head to the concrete pit floor. He rolls quickly over and drags Verez to the ground. He climbs on top of her.

"I hate cops, Bitch! You won't be the first Pig I've killed!" he confesses as he reaches for the gun.

Verez gets her arm loose and stabs her thumb into his eye so hard that she can feel it burst like a ripe grape. Diablo screams as Verez uses his recoil to roll with him and ends up fully mounted on top of him.

"I grew up to be just like my father! The only difference is I never forgot who you were!" Verez growls, before slamming a flurry of elbows down on the face and head of her father's killer until he is unconscious.

The fizzle of a cigarette's burning cherry can be heard through the silence of the crowd.

"That's a bad-ass bitch homes!" A voice calls out before the doors of the warehouse burst open and men in black gear rush into the building.

"FBI! Get to the ground! Now!" men order, M.P.5's in hand.

Outside Verez is being attended to by medical personnel when Blake Marshall and Rogers Hess walk to where she sits on the threshold of the rear open door of an ambulance.

"The good news, Xena, is that we have your man on organized dog fighting and unlicensed gambling. The bad news is none of the rest of the Aztec's are saying squat not even the one we untied," Blake informs her and Rogers nods his head with a sad smile. Verez waves the EMT away.

"He pointed a gun at a man's head!" she exclaims

Blake nods his head. "Okay, so we can add a reckless endangerment charge. Point is he'll be out next week, and they drowned your dog." Blake sticks it in and twists.

"What? Wait What? Why the hell would they do that?" she puts her hand to her head.

"He lost a ton of money for them. The good news is that he survived it. Bad news again, he's somewhere in Los Angeles," Blake continues.

"Great, so I have to do what now? Scour the city? Go door to door?" Verez feels as if she's failed,

"Or wait until he's mutilated a family pet?" Blake reasons.

"Or worse, a person or child!" Rogers says seriously. Verez and Blake look at one another gravely.

* * *

CHAPTER 39

When he wakes, it is to the sound of a robin singing nearby and the hum of a lawnmower in the distance. He stretches his powerful limbs, and his mouth opens wide, a high-pitched yawn escapes his throat. He is aware of a terrible ache in his right side. The grass is soft and a blade goes into his nose causing him to sneeze. His stomach aches from throbbing hunger but the thirst is worse. His tongue is swollen and dry and he smells water in the air.

Outside of the small playhouse, he moves cautiously toward a blue child's pool near steps that go up to the wooden deck of a large home. Neither the home nor the steps interest him. It is the water he is after and once his tongue begins lapping it does not stop until he is swollen with hydration.

Thirst quenched, he makes his way back to the shelter he has made his own. He lies back down in the cool grass and quickly dozes off. Far away from those who have used him for their own ends. The Brindle sleeps carefree not realizing that his presence was noticed and his return to the hiding spot observed. As he naps unknowingly, another mind is plotting on how to get him without raising any suspicions from those that might interfere with the ultimate plan.

His stalker is nearly upon him by the time he wakes and realizes he is cornered. For the playhouse, his shelter has become his trap and the only exit is being blocked by it. He leaps to his feet and a deep throated growl erupts from his slowly opening mouth but it does not faze the fearless creature that continues forward. He watches as it reaches into the box secured to its neck by a blood red string, and removes something.

The Brindle does not know what its intentions are, hasn't had time to smell its scent as he watches, whatever it has removed from the box, moves closer to his face. He opens his mouth to warn the creature one last time then suddenly the tiny fist stuffs a small animal cracker into his slightly open growling mouth - before another is stuck into his jaw to meet the fate of the one before it. He begins licking the hands of the small creature when the cookies have stopped coming. Then it happens. He smells it, the scent that makes him shiver and he sees only wonder and unconditional love. He doesn't know it, no, something much more than knowing, He feels it.

And not since that night, spent alone with his mother, has he felt such a warm pain in his chest. The child pets him over and over and in him, she feels as if a door has been opened and she's seeing the world around her for the first time. She does not know what it is she is petting, but the swirls of the colors of his fur remind her of the kitty she saw behind the glass in the place where the birds and fish were. "Kitty, nice kitty, kitty. Good kitty." Jasmine purrs as she pets his muscled shoulder.

He does not understand any of her words, but he knows that she is his and he is hers. He is no longer Ron Arwood's tool of destruction or Diablo's devil dog...he is now Jasmine's kitty. He is now in the world where he belongs. He steps closer and does something he has never done before. He licks the small soft face of the beautiful child, and she, in return, does what she has never done before. "Oh Kitty!" she giggles, and her eyes squint from the tickle of his tongue.

CHAPTER 40

He looks like the victim she thinks, as she stares at the gang leader from the dark room side of the two-way glass. A gauze and medical taped eye patch cover the left eye socket, and purple swollen bruises cover the right side of his face. Despite the loss of one eye, the venom in Diablo's gaze has not been lost. For two hours he has stared ahead, catatonically, at the glass as if somehow, he can see her, Rogers attempted to question him but none of the agent's accusations or threats elicited the slightest response.

"Maybe the bastards going for the insanity plea?" Blake guesses.

"Let me have a crack at 'em." Verez walks out of the observation room before either Blake or Rogers are able to object.

At first, when she enters, Diablo's demeanor remains unchanged, but as she sits across from where he is restrained to the metal chair he sits in, his one eye looks into one of hers. "You are all grown up now." He smiles warmly. It's all she can do not to shiver as the ice runs up her spine to her neck. "Yes, I remember you...what you said to me in the pit...that was what I told you that night." His smile becomes half a sneer..."

"So, you admit it? You admit you killed my father?" Verez nearly yells.

Diablo shakes his head. "I do not know what you are talking about agent, I've never killed anyone. I'm a business man." He smiles, as if to say you got nothing, Verez leans in close.

"I know you're a murderer. I may not be able to prove it but I know, and you know I know. I should have killed you in the pit." She whispers as she stares into his eye. He leans forward but is stopped by the restraints, his face only inches from her own, and sneers.

"I should have killed you that night. I was going to...I almost went back while you were there on the ground with him. If I could have reached my gun in the pit I would have killed you then." He whispers, but almost immediately realizes his mistake the moment the last few words leave his lips because Verez looks at the camera and back to the glass.

"You're right; we can't use anything you've said because your lawyer hasn't arrived. But the gun was evidence collected during a search supported by a warrant...can you say ballistics?" she stands and exits the interrogation room as Diablo curses and threatens her.

"Now why the hell didn't I think about that?" Blake asks as he and Rogers meet her in the hallway.

"So, what's next?" Rogers asks.

"Next, I find the dog, go back home and get another dirt ball off the streets." Verez rolls her eyes in exhaustion.

"It shouldn't be too hard to find the dog. An animal that violent, it's only a matter of time before that vicious monster does something to give us a lead on his location," Rogers says confidently.

Blake looks at Verez. "I wonder what that vicious bastard is doing right now."

CHAPTER 41

"Oh Carol, I'm sure it's all perfectly safe...he is a professional. Sarah walks into the kitchen, cell phone to her ear. She notices the back door is wide open and shuts it. "I don't know...a professional magician, tiger handler, a spandex wearer?" she laughs. She notices the open door but not the two faint paw prints leading from the door into the interior of the home or the subtle scent of motor oil. "Well, if we're going I better get Jazzy ready. Alright, hun, I'll see you there. Bye bye." She hangs the phone up and starts to call for her daughter but stops when she hears Jacob in his office.

Upstairs Jasmine and Kitty are playing in her large closet. The dog has a set of cat ears tied on his head like a bonnet and watches as the child dances stuffed animals around his front paws.

"Me-ow, me-ow kitty," the little girl giggles as the dog bends down and sniffs the toy cats. His cold wet nose rises to brush the child's cheek before his warm tongue licks her face. She drops the toys and wraps her arms around his calloused neck. He rubs his massive head gently against her sweet-smelling hair.

Downstairs, at that moment, Sarah enters Jacob's office while he talks with his studio CEO. "Jacob, will you be coming with us to Armondi's?" She asks, not caring that she's interrupting. Jacob turns around in his chair.

"I'm on the phone with Les, Sarah," Jacob scolds her.
"I'm sorry Les, I..." Jacob tries to apologize.

"Nonsense Jacob! How are you, Sarah?" Les asks from the conference call.

"I'm fine Les. We've been invited to a show. Armondi the Amazing is putting on for the children of the neighborhood." She speaks to the phone on the desk.

"That's great, Paula took the grand kids to see 'em in Vegas, said the guy is great! The kids loved 'em," Les informs as Jacob sighs. Les must have heard him. "Jacob get the hell out of that office for a while, get some fresh air and take your family to see the Great Armondi! That's and order!" Les laughs.

Sarah gets the feeling that she misjudged Les, believing him to be a slave driver and blaming him for keeping Jacob so busy. Jacob begins to object when Les continues. "Hey! I just got a great idea Jacob...why don't you bring Sarah and Jasmine down to the Island this weekend for the final shot of the film?"

Jacob looks at the phone and Sarah sees a look of horror on his face. His reaction breaks her heart but she keeps her poker face.

"I don't' want to drag them all the way down there for just two days," he looks at Sarah as if it's no big deal.

"You know as well as I do two days can become a week in this business. There's plenty of room on the jet and I'm sure Sarah could use a vacation?"

Les' idea becomes a question for Sarah who is doing good to hold tears back. Jacob turns back to his monitor.

"Let's discuss this alternate ending Les." Jacob reaches for a bound script.

"Don't let me and your daughter keep you from your work Jacob...who knows, maybe one day you'll have your own home to keep us out of your way instead of your own office room!" She slams the door as she walks out of the office. Jacob spins around in his chair, shocked by what his wife has just said.

With tears in her eyes, Sarah yells for her daughter, "Jasmine! Come on honey, we're going to see the big kitty cats! Let's go baby girl!"

In his office, Jacob does not know what to do. "She's in one of her moods." He says to Les but knows Sarah does not have moods like that.

"Let me tell you something I wish someone would have told me. We have the greatest job in the world son. The entertainment business is magic, we create worlds that bring families to movie theatres and around televisions to enjoy together, but I've been divorced twice and been to my son's third birthday party and his high school graduation, but I don't have a single memory in-between. I try to spend as much time with my grandchildren because life is too damn short son. If you love that woman and that child, get your ass out there and show them before it's no longer an option!" Jacob starts to say something but the dial tone interrupts him.

CHAPTER 42

Sarah makes her fourth pass around the golf course, nursery rhyme music playing over the radio, as she attempts to pull herself together. Between the third hole and the Caddie's Shack, she can look into Armondi's side yard and see children running around and playing and so she has time to make another pass and let the tears dry and the red in her cheeks and nose fade away before she arrives.

Part of her tears are due to guilt over what she had said to Jacob. How could she have said something like that? Was it a threat to shake him into getting his act together or did she mean it? Sarah wonders, not knowing herself. Panic grips her. What if he wants it that way? What if she just opened the door and he wants it and uses her words to justify leaving? What has she done? She wonders. As she gets past the third hole she can see that the children are all walking towards the magician's backyard. She looks into the mirror and is satisfied.

Moments later she is leading Jasmine around the side of Armondi's house when she finds Carol waiting at the open gate.

"I was getting worried about you two, Jacob said that you'd make it through." Carol bends down and kisses Jasmine's head.

Sarah starts to inquire about her having spoken to Jacob but she decides she must have called the house and he answered the phone. "I wanted to drive around the neighborhood a little while and see how everyone's doing." Sarah fibs.

"Well, ya missed 'em because they're all here just about. Come on before we miss the new cat Armondi the Amazing just brought back from Vegas," Carol turns and leads them back.

Sarah sees that most every family that's appeared at the show is there in their entirety, mother and father, accompanying their children. She knows the questions she will get from Abby, Samantha, and Charlotte and she knows what she will say..." Jacob wants to come, but he's so swamped with the new movie and..." her prepared excuse is cut short as she reaches the row of chairs, where the Hertzle's are to be seated, to find Jacob already there.

There is a look on his face, and because they have been together so long, and know each other so well, she gives him a look to respond to his own. He says. "I'm sorry." She says, "Me too." Each knows what the other means.

"Would you be available for a weekend, which may become a week or two, in the Virgin Islands?" he asks as Armondi takes the stage.

"I'll have to get someone to fix the alarm," She informs him as she helps Jasmine into her seat.

"I'll take a look at it."

Sarah gives him a sideways look.

"What? I'll take a look at it." He promises.

"No, I'll have someone who knows what they're doing look at it. You still have to look at the clogged drain in the washroom, and there is also a tree branch that's crashed through the fence in the backyard for you to look at." She grows quieter as Armondi's assistant brings the tiger out onto the stage.

"I'll put a posting on the computer and have it done before Friday." She whispers. Jacob leans in. "I'll be working most of the time we're on the Island but you and Jasmine can see the sights and have a wonderful time." He smiles.

"As long as you and I have a little time. We need to talk Jacob." She says seriously.

"We will...I promise."

The show is great, the children of the neighborhood along with most of the parents, appear to be thoroughly entertained but the Hertzle's each seem to be preoccupied with other things. If one could read minds they would find Jacob wondering what Sarah was wanting to talk about and fearing the prospect of a divorce. Sarah, on the other hand, wonders how to go about broaching the delicate subject that perhaps Jacob feels uncomfortable around their child. Meanwhile, Jasmine's mind is four blocks away, in the closet of her room.

CHAPTER 43

The evening after Armondi the Amazing performs for the neighborhood families, Sarah posts an ad on the internet requesting the services of anyone capable of security system maintenance, within forty-eight hours she receives two responses, makes a choice as to whom she will hire and is fixing the young man a glass of iced tea as he works. She enters the living room with the tea to find Rusty, the security system repair man, securing the alarm face panel back on the wall mounted system. He turns to her before accepting the glass.

"That should do it Mrs. Hertzle. Let's have the code, and we'll run a diagnostics test," he explains.

She gives him the seven-digit code, which she informs him, is her daughter's date of birth and he punches the numbers on the keyboard of the alarm. A red light flickers on in the corner of the panel.

"That's a good sign," Sarah says seeing the red light on for the first time in months.

Rusty slowly opens the door when a loud series of beeps begin. He pushes in the code once more, and the alarm goes silent. He repeats the process on the window and back door before he seems satisfied that the problem has been corrected. Sarah is delighted as she pays him.

"I feel so much better. It's been months since it broke. Now, with us leaving for the Islands. Well, I can rest easy now," she explains.

"So, you're on vacation soon? That's cool." The baby-faced tech savvy young man says.

"It's not really a vacation. My husband is in the film industry, and it's for his job, but we're leaving Friday and we could come back Sunday evening or two weeks after...you never know with his work?" She smiles.

"Well, if you have any more problems Mrs. Hertzle just call the number I gave you and I'll come back and take care of it," he looks around the home and Sarah thinks he's wanting to leave but doesn't want to be rude.

"I will Rusty, and thanks again," she opens the door to show him out, and he thinks she's a rude stuck-up Bitch who can't wait for the help to be out of her home.

He walks out with a pleasant smile. "Goodbye Mrs. Hertzle."

"Take care, Rusty," she calls to him.

She is about to shut the door when she sees Jacob's car pulling into the drive. Rusty waves to Jacob as he gets into his white compact car. Jacob returns the wave as he shuts his car door and looks puzzled up at Sarah.

"He just finished fixing the alarm," she smirks at her husband as he comes up the steps. Sarah sees a look on his face that she does not like.

"A tropical thunderstorm is hitting the Islands," he says apologetically, as he comes through the door.

"So, the trip is off?" she asks already knowing the answer.

"Just until after the weather gets better." He closes the door and kisses her forehead.

"When will that be exactly?" Sarah asks walking to the bottom of the steps. "It's hurricane season so...it could be a little while,"

Sarah rolls her eyes before looking up the stairs and calling for her daughter.

"Jasmine Marie! It's time to get cleaned up for supper honey. Come down stairs!" Jasmine hears her mother from where she lays, her head upon Kitty's chest as the dog lies on its side, in her closet. Jasmine gets up.

"Stay Kitty," she whispers in the dogs cropped ear.

Kitty turns and licks the child's face which causes the little girl to giggle in delight before getting up and walking out of the closet, shutting the door behind her.

Kitty stares at the closed closet door, until the child's footsteps fade away, before laying on his side and wallowing into the softness of the carpet. It's his first time experiencing carpet. The concrete foundations of the Southern Georgia kennel and the Aztec warehouse were his only beds.

He wallows deeper into the shag floor and exhales deeply, it is good to him and beat out only by the warm, soft embrace of the child. Warm and soft, things he had never experienced. Cold and hard was everything in his life until he met her.

No kicks but kisses, instead of hitting there is hugs, and in place of the cold hard chains around his scarred neck, it is now her warm, soft little arms. Her warmth has penetrated into his broad chest and awakened the memory he had all but forgotten. A faded picture in his head of a night spent, face-to-face, with another who wanted nothing more than to love him.

He knows he will never allow anything to happen to this child, not as long as there is air in his lungs or a beat in his heart.

Downstairs she walks between her mother and her father who both bend down to kiss her.

"Whew! Jasmine." Her mother comments on the child's smell. "We have to get you a bath child. Where have you been playing?" Sarah takes the girl to the bathroom.

"Does she smell like motor oil to you?" Jacob watches Sarah as she washes the child's hands and face with soap and water.

"More like a wet horse." Sarah dries Jasmine with a towel. "We're getting straight in the tub after supper little girl."

At the table Jacob edits a script, highlighting the areas that need to be changed or taken out completely. Sarah wipes the counter down and hears a soft voice. She turns to see Jacob looking equally surprised at Jasmine who pushes her spoon around the macaroni. "Me-ow me-ow me-ow kitty." The child chants softly not looking up from her plate. Jacob looks up at Sarah who smiles back at him.

"Kitty kitty." Jasmine giggles and Sarah nearly weeps upon hearing her daughter laugh.

After Jasmine has been bathed and put to bed, Sarah and Jacob sit awake in their bed. "Do you think it was the tiger Sarah...she said kitty?" Jacob wonders.

Sarah shakes her head slowly. "She's been acting different the last few days...I don't know why but she has," she says.

Jacob frowns. "Well today is the first I've noticed it," he snaps back.

"That's not hard to believe. How could you notice from the studio or closed up in your office until she's in bed every night?" Sarah lays back on the bed.

"What the hell are you saying?" Jacob turns to his wife.

"I'm saying that for all the time you are around her how would you know how she's doing? She's your daughter. Autism is not contagious Jacob. Don't worry you won't catch it if you spend a few minutes around her every once in a while!" Sarah decides to lay it all out.

Jacob looks stunned and then angry but before he can snap back at her, a look of guilt falls over his face. His shoulders sag and Sarah realizes that that was not at all broaching the subject delicately.

"Jacob I'm sorry. I did not mean it like...," she begins to apologize, but he cuts her off.

"No. No, you're right Sarah. I've been a complete coward. It's not that I feel like I could catch Autism. Nothing so absurd. But I don't know, like I might be responsible for her having it?" he turns away and Sarah raises up and moves closer to him.

"I went through that for a time too, but since, I've learned a lot about Autism and it's like the doctor said. It's completely random." She leans her head on his shoulder.

He takes a deep breath. "How do I face her now? I feel like the biggest piece of crap ever...I've been avoiding my own child because I'm scared?" he shakes his head.

"She doesn't know why you've not been around honey, but I know she knows you've been gone. You face her by facing her. She' going to be more forgiving than you can imagine. I bet she won't even bring it up?" Sarah laughs which causes Jacob to laugh as well.

Down the hall, just out of range of their voices as they talk in bed. Jasmine's bed is empty. Her closet door shut and inside the child is laying down. Head on the resting ribs of Kitty.

The child has never felt more comfortable, and the dog never more loved or at genuine peace. Each has found in the other, what both had been without their entire lives. Each is the other's missing piece and neither will let go without a fight.

CHAPTER 44

Blake walks into the conference room, which Verez has turned into her temporary office, and drops a manila envelope on the table in front of her. Verez removes the contents and begins reading.

"The ballistics show a conclusive match from the rifling on the "Reaper" and the slugs removed from three bodies so far," he explains.

Verez finds what she is looking for, as Blake says it. "One of them being that of Raul Verez." He pats her shoulder before walking out of the room so that she may have a moment alone.

Though she made no vows to find her father's killer, and honestly never thought it would be possible to do so after all these years, she feels as if something more than fate allowed for her to cross paths with him. There is a sense of completion that she feels for the very first time in her life, but almost immediately it is followed by the knowledge that the dog is still somewhere out wondering Los Angeles and Vance is back in Atlanta running the city.

One step at a time, she tells herself. The city animal shelter has turned up nothing, and none of the half dozen reported dog bites have been from the Brindle pit bull. Perhaps Rogers is right? Sitting back and waiting for the dog to show its colors may be the only way to get a bead on its location? How long, she wonders, will that possibly be?

* * *

CHAPTER 45

The house is silent in the darkness of night. Jacob lays curled up on his side of his section of the queen-sized mattress. Sarah is sprawling wide in her sleep taking the rest of the bed and all of the blankets while she gently snores.

In the closet of her bedroom, Jasmine sleeps curled next to the dog that sleeps peacefully with his large head upon a crushed box of finger paints.

The house is silent until a quiet cracking sound comes from the small window beside the front door. A gloved hand which pushes through the small opening and reaches up to the keyboard of the security alarm and begins punching numbers. The hand slides to the door and unlocks the dead bolt. Slowly and silently, the front door opens, and two shadowy figures enter the home closing the door back, quietly, behind them.

Upstairs Jasmine wakes, exits the closet and shuts the door behind her. The little girl walks from her room into the bathroom across the hall and closes the door just as the two figures move past and down the hall to her parent's room.

"I thought she said they would be gone!" one whispers to the other.

"Let's get the hell out of here." The other says and turns to leave.

"No, we're already here. Let's just tie them up and do what we came to do!" he grabs his partner's arm.

By the time Jacob realizes the men are there, a knife is to his throat, and he does as he's told for fear of his family's safety. Sarah complies as well and they allow themselves to be bound by the strips of sheet the men rip from their bed. As the two men take the couple downstairs, Jasmine exits the bathroom and one of the men scoops the child up into his arms and takes her to the lower level with her parents.

After securing Jasmine alongside of her parents on the floor of the living room and pulling the curtains closed, one of the men turns on a lamp light.

"What the hell are you doing?" the other man yells and Sarah can see that it is the young man that fixed the security alarm.

"Rusty!" she exclaims.

Rusty looks at the other man in disbelief.

"It doesn't matter...it's not your real name and you gave 'er a track phone number...it can't be traced back to you." The brown-haired man says. His teeth are yellow and his skin is oily.

"I still didn't want them seeing our faces!" Rusty explains.

"Well if you're too worried about it we can always make sure they don't ever tell anyone anything?" yellow teeth shows the knife.

"You're crazy! Hell no! Let's just get what we can and get the hell out of here. I'll start in the back..." Rusty is interrupted by Jasmine.

"Kitty! Want Kitty!" the child nearly cries. Rusty's cold hard look melts instantly as he kneels down beside the little girl.

"Oh honey, where is Kitty?" he asks, brushing his hand over her head.

"Room...Kitty in room." She looks up at him, and the tears in her bright blue eyes remind him of his little sister and how he could never say no to her.

"Go upstairs to the kid's room and get her cat!" Rusty orders.

"Are you kiddin?" he asks. "Get her, her cat!"

"It's upstairs in her room! Now!" he orders.

"You're not cut out for this shit man!"

Through yellow teeth he complains as he goes up the stairs. Sarah and Jacob look at one another in confusion.

"Make this easy on us so we can get out of here. Where do you keep the money and your good jewelry?" Rusty asks Jacob and Sarah.

Upstairs yellow teeth walks into Jasmine's room and turns the light on. "Where the hell are you cat? Here Kitty, Kitty, Kitty...I can't believe I'm doing this sh...," he hears something in the closet and walks to the door. "Come here cat before I wring you damn neck!" he opens the door to discover that Kitty is not at all what he expected.

Downstairs, Jacob is explaining that they keep very little money in the home and Sarah is not a big jewelry person, when yellow teeth's scream causes everyone to freeze.

"What kind of cat do you have kid?" Rusty asks Jasmine.

Yellow teeth dashes down the stairs and dives through the window at the bottom of the steps. Hot on his trail, Kitty reaches the bottom step and sees Rusty standing over Jasmine.

A deep throated growl seems to shake the entire house as Rusty runs to the window yellow teeth dove through, moments earlier, and jumps but does not make it, Kitty's massive jaws clamp down on his buttocks. Rusty howls in pain as Kitty shakes his powerful head side to side. Rusty's pants rip and he falls to the ground below. The terrified crook hobbles off holding his backside and has no clue that he has left his wallet on the ground below the broken window.

The dog turns back around and walks to the family as the sounds of approaching sirens grows louder. Sarah and Jacob freeze in fear as the ugly pit bull walks closer to where they sit helplessly and bound by strips of sheet. As the dog moves toward Jasmine, Sarah yells at it. No! Go! You go! Get away from her!" she screams. The dog turns in surprise by the intensity in Sarah's voice.

Car doors slam shut. Several police, guns drawn, enter the home. Kitty stands guard over Jasmine and her family and thinks about the red pit bull that day in the pit. How it feared for the human. Kitty is prepared to defend the child from these men.

"Call your dog off if you want us to untie you!" one officer explains.

"It's not our dog!" Jacob yells.

* * *

CHAPTER 46

Diablo, Flaco and several other Aztecs sit at a table in the Los Angeles detention center. Several other inmates are standing around watching television.

"The ballistics came back. My attorney says I'm looking at, at least three bodies right now. That means I'm pretty much hit but the rest of you will be back out soon and you, Flaco, you will be the man out there." Diablo passes the torch and Flaco nods his head.

The Aztec's listening could not be happier but keep grave looks upon their faces.

"I am tired and my pain medication is kicking in. We will speak more in the morning but you all need to be prepared because you will be back on the streets in a few months and the Aztecs will have to get our respect back. Fan must be dealt with and Gordo, if he can be found. We will talk more tomorrow. I'm heading to bed." Diablo leaves them. They all look at Flaco, waiting for him to speak.

"I'm not as strict as Diablo but there will not be any stupidity tolerated. We will take care of Fan and take Parkview back, but the dog fighting...that is over with. I also have plans on turning some of our bad money into good money. Legitimate business." Flaco informs them.

Pito, the smart ass, looks up. "You gonna incorporate the Aztecs?"

"As a matter of fact, I just might." Flaco smiles.

"Hey, check this out!" One of the other inmates turns the volume up on the television. A news reporter speaks as three animal rescue officers struggle to pull a brindle colored pit bull towards their truck.

"Channel eight has learned that the dog that saved the family from the burglary is actually not their dog but rather a stray." The woman talks into the mic as the camera shows the dog fighting with the rescue workers.

Flaco recognizes Perro del Diablo and smiles. "That's a bad ass dog homes!" he says as he watches the dog before the scene cuts away to a neighbor talking to the camera.

"Damn thing became a superhero. He's out there saving people and shit." Pito starts making everyone laugh.

The kid is funny, Flaco thinks. And he is very smart. Perhaps he might make a good right-hand man? Perro del Diablo has found his way, he thinks, there is no way a dog hero won't be adopted by someone. Good luck my friend. He smiles as the dog is shown once more. He laughs as Pito continues his free style stand-up routine.

CHAPTER 47

The house is alive with activity as detectives take pictures and repair men work on everything from the broken window to the security alarm. Every few minutes someone from the neighborhood stops by to either check in to see if they are alright, give advice about security agencies or leave a dinner dish.

Jacob walks into the kitchen rubbing his head. "We might have been better off with the burglars." He moans.

"Tell me about it. One more green bean casserole and the table legs are going to give out." She sets a glass dish in the only open space available on the table.

Two men stop at the kitchen door. "Excuse us but do either of you recognize this guy?" one of the detectives asks holding an open wallet so that Sarah and Jacob can see the photo ID.

"That's Rusty!" Sarah steps forward to get a closer look.

The name under the picture says Randall Rogers.

"So this is the burglar you knew to be Rusty?" the older detective with the wallet asks.

"That's the guy." Jacob answers for his wife.

"You said that your daughter asked for her kitty? The other guy went to get it, but the dog showed up and chased them off. Have either of you seen the cat since?" the younger detective asks.

"That's the thing, we don't have a cat. No animals with fur can be in the house. Jasmine and Jacob are both allergic to pet dander." Sarah explains.

"So was she, Jasmine, asking for maybe a stuffed animal or something?" the older detective asks.

"She does have a bunch of stuffed cats?" Jacob shrugs.

"If you'll excuse me I have to go clean her room. She'll be home from school in a few hours." Sarah smiles as she leaves the men in the kitchen.

"We'll get these guys Mr. Hertzle. I don't think it'll be too much trouble tracking down this master mind." The officer holds the wallet up for emphasis.

Upstairs, Sarah picks a few of Jasmine's toys up and set them on her toy box. She makes the bed and happens to glance through the open closet door. Inside she finds empty sandwich meat wrappers and a soup bowl half full of water. It's not until she discovers dry hard feces, stuck to the carpet that everything begins to make sense. Downstairs, Jacob is about to enter his office when Sarah yells his name.

"Jacob! Come up here!" his wife calls, and by the tone of her voice he realizes something is wrong. He walks into Jasmine's room to find Sarah kneeling down in the closet.

"Hey, that's where my deli meat went." Jacob sees the empty wrappers.

Sarah looks back at him. "This is where she kept him." She holds the bowl up.

"Kept who?" Jacob asks.

"Kitty. This is where she kept the dog, Jacob. The dog is Kitty!" she laughs.

"You mean Jasmine had that thing in our house?" he sits down on the child's bed.

"Yes, and we have to get it back." Sarah stands with the bowl in her hands. Jacob looks up at her as if she's lost her mind.

"Are you crazy? Did you see that thing? It looks like a gargoyle without wings! No Sarah! We don't know where it's been! We don't know what it's capable of." He shakes his head. Sarah kneels down in front of him.

"The last few days Jasmine's been so much better. We heard her laugh Jacob. It's because of kitty. We know where it's been. She motions toward the closet and look at how happy she's been. We know exactly what it's capable of." Sarah pleads and Jacob looks at her before he nods his head slowly.

CHAPTER 48

Jacob watches Jasmine, feet swinging, as she sits alongside him in the waiting area of the Orange County Animal Shelter. The line is long, and it's nearly an hour before their number is called. At the counter, Jacob can see the receptionist is having a long day.

"Can I help you?" she asks with a look of complete disinterest.

"Ah, yes...we're here about a dog." Jacob holds Jasmine on his hip.

"The blue form is for lost dogs and the yellow is to adopt a dog. Which would you like sir?" she still has not looked at him as she pulls one of each form from beneath the counter.

"Well, actually we're wanting a dog that came in last night." Jacob swings Jasmine from one hip to the other.

"Does your dog have a collar, a tattoo or a tracking capsule?" she grabs the phone preparing to call someone.

"See, it's not exactly our dog but he came in last night and we'd like to get it..."

"Sir, she interrupts, last night was Friday and over a hundred dogs came in. I'm sure we wouldn't know the dog you are talking about unless it has some sort of identifying traits; like a collar, tattoo or capsule. So, if it's an adoption you want..."

"It's a brindle colored dog with hardly any ears and it looks like a gargoyle without wings!" Jacob interrupts her. She is about to give a trained automatic response when a look of recognition comes to her face.

"Oh, I know the dog you're talking about. Come with me sir." She walks to the door and opens it so that he and Jasmine can follow her towards the back.

Walking down the rows of caged dogs in one section of the shelter. Jacob is immediately struck by the silence and the receptionist seems to read his mind.

"It's usually so loud in here...it's almost like they are all afraid of him...I've never seen anything like it?" she shakes her head.

Turning down one final row, to where the larger cages are. Jacob lets Jasmine down when he sees the brindle colored pit bull laying on its side facing the wall. The food and water in its cage appears untouched.

"He's been lying here like that the whole time. Won't drink or eat anything." She explains, Jasmine sees the dog and dashes to the cage.

"Kitty!" the child screams reaching her small arms into the cage.

Jacob is struck with panic as the dog leaps and rushes towards the child. He starts to pull her back but it's too late, the pit bull is upon her allowing her to hug him as it licks her face hastily through the cage.

"Oh kitty!" she laughs while the dog licks her face over and over. Jacob's eyes fill and overflow as he watches his daughter laugh and snuggle up to the ugliest dog he has ever seen.

"You'd have to see it to believe it." The woman wipes tears from her own eyes, "It's like beauty and the beast...literally!" she exclaims reaching for napkins in her pocket. She gives one to Jacob and keeps one for herself as both watch and wipe while the dog and girl greet each other as if they are the only two in the large room. It's several minutes before the reunion is interrupted but the woman is so taken by the passion between the Autistic child and the stray pit bull that she cuts through most of the red tape and allows for Jacob and Jasmine to take Kitty home within an hour.

Sarah meets them as soon as they enter the home. "Look at the scars. What has that poor thing been through?" Sarah asks Jacob as they watch Jasmine walk beside Kitty as the dog walks around the living room smelling the couches.

"Whatever happened to it, it didn't make him mean. And it's strong as an ox." He comments as the dog pushes the couch several inches away from the wall.

"We have to get it a bath." Sarah waves the stench away.

"There's the motor oil and wet horse we were wondering about." He laughs.

The first attempt to get Kitty into the bath tub ends with Jacob being drug down the hall. The second, Sarah goes with him as Kitty takes them both into Jasmine's room. The third is a success as Jacob enters the bathroom, sleeves rolled up, ready for round three. He finds Kitty in the tub along with Jasmine. Sarah looks up at him and raises her eyebrows.

"I figured if this didn't work we'd have to walk Kitty through an automatic car wash." She laughs.

Jacob kneels down and begins washing Jasmine as Sarah washes the dog shakes sending soap and water all over them. For the first time, all three laugh together and it feels so natural that neither Jacob nor Sarah recognized this milestone. They are, for the first time, finally a family.

Later as she lays in bed, nearly asleep, recounting the day's events, Sarah will realize how great this day was. But for now, as they are soaked and laughing, they are living life and loving every second. Enjoying the moment and thinking of nothing else.

THE BRINDLE

* * *

CHAPTER 49

Verez enters the Orange County Animal Shelter and walks to the counter. "Excuse me, but I'd like to speak with the supervisor." She says to the woman who had helped Jacob and Jasmine when they had come for Kitty.

"I'm afraid you're going to have to wait in line like everyone else miss." The receptionist explains.

Verez removes her ID from her pocket and shows the woman. "Special Agent Dominica Verez, of the FBI. Now can I speak with the supervisor?" Verez clinches her teeth.

The woman reaches beneath the counter and removes a shirt pin and attaches it to her shirt before pointing at it. "Supervisor Daniel Singleton, of the Orange County Animal Shelter. Now please find a seat special agent Verez there are six people ahead of you." The supervisor points to the waiting area.

Verez turns and walks over to the seats and plops down in one. A young man smiles at her and shakes his head.

"She's serious when it comes to this job." The young man laughs.

"You'd think an agent on official business might get a pass?" Verez watches the supervisor, who finishes with a young couple before calling an elderly woman to the counter next.

"I'm not too surprised, I'm just here to get the spare key, and she's making me wait. I lost mine back at the campus and can't get in the house." The young man explains.

Verez looks at him, her bewilderment is obvious.

"She's my mother. I've been here over half an hour already...I'm last, or I was until you came in." The supervisor's son smiles before he and Verez both start laughing.

Verez's phone rings. "Hello?" She tries to compose herself.

"That you Verez? You crying?" Blake asks from the other end.

"No! I'm laughing." She informs him. "Well, where are you? He asks.

"I'm at the Orange County Animal Shelter where the channel eight news people said the dog from the home invasion is," she explains watching an old man being called to the counter.

"That footage was from two weeks ago Verez...someone probably claimed him, or they've already put him down by now?" Blake explains.

"Well, I'm about to find out what's going on. Do you need me?" Verez sees a woman and child take the old man's place.

The supervisor's son mouths. "I'm next!" with a ridiculous amount of excitement. Verez shakes her head.

"No, you're good...where are you at? I just thought that you'd want to know that Diablo's dead." He informs her.

"Wait, what? How?" Verez is shocked.

"Three of the other three bodies on Reaper...they were the three other original Aztecs we all assumed he had them killed to take the gang over as the one and only leader, but we never guessed he killed them all himself. Well, the prosecutor announced the three new charges, and the victims, in open court. Diablo was stabbed to death three hours later in his holding cell." Blake explains.

"Do we know who killed him?" she asks stunned by the news.

"Two Asians of the Asian connection," Blake says quickly.

"Won't that start a war or something?" Verez cannot believe the devil is dead.

"We think it's probably a favor or debt payment between gangs. Either way, Diablo got his judgment, I guess. Are you okay?" he asks genuinely concerned.

"Yeah, I mean it's kind of like an end after all these years...even more than arresting and charging him was. I guess I don't have to worry about a jury or technicality." She says.

"No, he's been tried, convicted, and executed. It's a wrap. We can go get a few drinks after work if you'd like...that's not an attempt at asking for a date, just..." Blake tries to explain.

"I know Blake, and I appreciate it, but I'll be pretty busy for the next few days, and that's how I get through things, but thanks." She says.

He gets it. "Alright Verez, but if you need anything, don't hesitate to ask." He offers.

"I won't. Thanks, Blake." She ends the conversation and waves at the supervisor's son who holds up the key on his way out.

Verez walks to the counter and supervisor Singleton smiles at her.

"Now how can I help you agent?" she asks without the slightest hint of attitude which in anyone else, Verez would have read as cocky, but having waited beside the woman's son, she realizes that Daniel Singleton is an orderly person.

"Yes, I'm looking for this dog, Verez pulls out the tablet and shows the woman a still frame of the bridle before the Hector fight, "Have you still got him?" she asks.

Verez sees the instant look of recognition on the woman's face followed by a smile. An almost warm smile, Verez thinks.

"I'm sorry but the animal has been placed with a family already," the supervisor explains.

"Can I please have their contact information?" Verez asks.

"I'm sorry, but unless you have a court order compelling me to turn over that kind of information, I cannot give it to you." The woman states matter of fact like. Verez feels her temperature rise but takes a moment before responding.

"I can do that. I can, but it will take a day or two..." the woman starts to say something but Verez holds her hand up nearly touching the supervisor's face. Daniel sees the look in Verez's eyes and decides to hear her out, "...but, by that time it may be too late.

Now, I'm assuming that the family had children?" Verez asks.

The supervisor nods her head, and Verez realizes that she's reaching the woman and decides to let her tablet finish Mrs. Singleton off. Verez hits play and footage of the fight begins. Within twenty minutes Verez is on her way to the home of Jacob Hertzle.

As she drives, she thinks of her father's killer being brutally stabbed to death in a prison cell. If asked about it she would say that it was wrong and those responsible deserved the most severe punishment. That's what she would say if asked, but she feels very different. She feels as if she is breathing for the first time in over twenty years. She hopes that the evil gang lord who called himself Diablo was now, at this moment, facing the real devil in hell and having to answer for trademark infringement. She hopes the punishment had something to do with pineapples being stuffed in a certain orifice for all eternity. She had seen Hitler receive the same sort of punishment in a movie and hopes he and Diablo are stock partners in hell. She laughs to herself as she continues along following the directions of the GPS.

Verez realizes that she has changed a great deal since Diablo's arrest. The last time she really laughed was as a child, it was the last time the world had been a good enough place to find anything humorous for her, but today already she has found two things "Laughy" as Ryan had said. She laughs out loud this time when she recalls what the instructor had said that day. As the giggles pass, she starts to think about the day and how she hopes that she isn't too late. What the hell are the parents thinking, Verez wonders. What the hell are they thinking?

CHAPTER 50

Jacob, Sarah, and Jasmine are walking Kitty around the neighborhood when an SUV pulls alongside of them. The driver side window rolls down, and Jacob recognizes Jason Court.

"Hey Jacob, Sarah, how are you guys doing?" Jason asks.

"Hi Sarah!" Jason's wife, Mary, leans over her husband to greet Sarah.

"Hi Mary!" Sarah waves. Mary looks down at Jasmine.

"Hey Jazzy baby. What do you have there? Oh dear, look at him, Jason." Mary sees Kitty.

"Holy cow, Jacob! What laboratory did you get that thing from?" Jason asks.

"Kitty is the dog that saved us from the people that broke into our home a few weeks ago. Jasmine loves him and the dog can't stand being away from her. We decided to keep him." Jacob looks down at the dog.

Kitty catches a scent pushed out of the Court's vehicle by the air conditioning through the open window. He does not understand why but the smell is causing his mind to race and his mouth to water.

"Let me pull into the driveway Jacob. I have something I want the two of you to see." Jason says as he starts to drive ahead.

"Bye Sarah." Mary leans over Jason.

"For God's sake Mary, we're just parking, you can talk to her!" Jason complains. Jacob and Sarah laugh as they walk towards the Court's driveway.

Jason gets out and walks to where the Hertzle's wait on the side of the street

Kitty sniffs Jason's shoes and pants, the scent is very strong on the man. He reaches down and pets the dog's head.

"Jesus, it's like petting and anvil with fur, this thing is strong." Jason wonders as he looks the dog over.

"What I was wanting to talk to you about, Jason points to a huge pile of dirt next to an old white pickup truck, is that eye sore right there!" Jacob notices the pile for the first time, it's about nine feet high and dwarf's the pickup truck between it and Jason's eight-foot privacy fence a few feet away from the truck.

"What is Frank doing?" Jacob asks looking at the huge pile of dirt.

"He's putting in a pool and the cheap skate figures to save money by digging the hole himself. Look at it Jacob, it's been there two months now and grass is starting to grow on top of the dirt...Frank never finishes anything, he's on his fourth marriage." Jason jibs.

"Well, you can't fault the guy for wanting to save a little money?" Jacob defends.

Mary leads a white pit bull from the back of the SUV. Kitty sees the dog and begins dragging Jacob towards it.

"Mary! For God's sake, get Lamb in the back yard! Hurry!" Jason yells as he attempts to help Jacob restrain Kitty.

The smell reaches kitty and his mind goes blank save the desire to reach the other dog.

"She's in heat and he smells it too, it's like holding a Buick back! That things a monster!" Jason leans down and pets Kitty.

The dog's eyes roll as he searches for the female before spotting her through the thin spaces of the wooden privacy fence. Kitty watches intently as Lamb paces the fence on her side. "You can't get to her now boy, not unless you can jump over an eight foot fence!" Jason informs Kitty, before continuing the conversation with Jacob.

As the two men talk Kitty concentrates on Lamb. There is no opening for him to squeeze through, he sees that very quickly. He scans the perimeter of the fence before noticing the truck beside the fence, and then he looks at the pile of dirt only a few feet from the truck. The dirt pile to the cab of the truck and from the truck's cab to the top of the fence. His body quivers Jacob feels the strain on the leash.

"We have to go to the co-op with this; he's bringing the value of all our homes down," Jason complains.

"Maybe something came up? He's probably going to finish it? Just give him a little time." Jacob defends Frank's procrastination and feels Sarah's eyes on him. The Court's front door opens and Mary pokes her head out.

"Jason! Your mother's on the phone. She said something about water pipes in the basement bursting and baseball cards!" Mary relays the message.

"I have a Nolan Ryan rookie card there!" Jason turns and quickly makes his way to the house.

"We'll talk later Jacob?" he yells over his shoulder as he walks inside.

"I noticed how you defended Frank. A little close to home, huh?" Sarah laughs.

"I'll fix the washroom sink, probably take a bottle of drain cleaner, that's all." Jacob shrugs.

"The busted fence in the backyard's going to take more than a bottle of anything." She tugs on his hand as they walk. Kitty turns back a few times to look at the dirt pile and fence.

"Mary Lamb'...Mary Little Lamb." Jasmine sings, and Sarah smiles.

She remembers the day she spoke to the principal outside of the classroom. The other children sang Mary had a Little Lamb while Jasmine appeared to be oblivious to everything around her, but now Sarah realizes she was always there. Sarah bends down and pets Kitty. Thank you. She says to herself, as if he understands. Kitty looks up into Sarah's eyes.

When they arrive at home, Sarah stops. "How about you take Jasmine and Kitty to the backyard while I fix lunch." She bends down and kisses Jasmine's head.

"You two want to go play around back?" Jacob pets the dog.

"While you are back there you can look at the fence and see what it's going to take to fix it." Sarah walks towards the front door and Jacob takes Jasmine and Kitty around the side of the house.

"Yes, dear." Jacob calls back.

As Sarah starts up the steps to the front door a dark blue sedan pulls into the driveway and she stops to see who it is. An attractive Hispanic woman gets out of the car. The woman has a leather satchel and fire arm on her side.

"Mrs. Hertzle?" the woman asks.

"Yes, I'm Sarah Hertzle" Sarah opens the front door.

"I'm Special Agent Dominica Verez. Would you mind if I spoke with you for a moment?" Verez asks showing Sarah her identification.

"No, please come inside."
In the living room Sarah motions for Verez to take a seat on the couch.

"Would you like something to drink Miss Verez?" Sarah offers.

"No, thank you." Verez declines.

"How can I help you Miss Verez?" she inquires.

"I've just left the Orange County Animal Shelter and your husband, Jacob adopted a brindle colored pit bull?" Verez asks.

"Yes, Kitty. He saved us from some men that broke into our home. He's a part of our family, why?" Sarah asks suspiciously.

"I'm aware that you have a child Mrs. Hertzle and I don't know what kind of dog you think Kitty is, but I assure you that this animal is dangerous. It was trained to be a killer and judging by the men who have helped raise it, and men who've killed for the dog, I'd say that it is very good at doing just that. As a mother, I'd think your daughter should come first and foremost." Verez implores Sarah but finds a nerve.

"Are you a mother Miss Verez?" Sarah asks with a fire in her eyes.

"No, but I..."

"Then don't come into my home telling me how to be one!" Sarah fires back.

Verez decides to go back to old reliable and pulls the tablet out of her satchel.
"I want you to see something Mrs. Hertzle. I believe it will give you an idea of what this dog, you call Kitty, is capable of." Verez sets the tablet and plays the fight.

She watches Sarah's facial expressions as she witnesses the brindle destroy the bigger dog.

"Do you understand what just happened Sarah? Did you see how easily he killed that other dog?" Verez asks as Sarah wipes the tears from her eyes. She knows the footage has saved the day again.

"Yes, I understand what happened...I understand what Kitty has been through now. That's what makes him so amazing, how he could be treated so horribly for so long and still be the kind of dog that he is." Sarah attempts to compose herself.

"He killed that dog Sarah, as easily as someone might step on a bug. He's a killer, don't you understand that?" Verez attempts to get through to the woman.

"What I understand is he is a survivor. I won't pretend to know a great deal about the world that Kitty came from. I live a very sheltered and privileged life, but I've seen shows on TV that talk about how these animals are mistreated and made to fight. What choice did Kitty have but to kill Miss Verez? What would have happened to him if he had not fought?" Sarah asks and Verez is left unable to argue, but instead goes back to the basics

"He has been trained to kill Sarah, he's dangerous and I don't think you understand what he is capable of! Think about your daughter and what a dog like that is capable of doing to her." Verez feels as if she still has a chance at winning the woman over.

Sarah goes silent and Verez knows that the mother is seeing the light.

"I've seen your video Miss Verez, if you wouldn't mind. I'd like to show you one of my own." Sarah stands and walks to the flat screen and going into the cabinet beneath the television removes a DVD.

This can't be good for the team, Verez decides. When the disc begins playing a little girl sits in front of a small cake with two candles on it. Sarah blows out the candles as the child looks on emotionlessly.

"That's Jasmine's second birthday," Sarah says before pushing a button on the remote.

The screen flashes and the girl sits in front of a cake and the only things that have changed are the three candles and the girl has gotten bigger.

"That's her third and the fourth is the same Miss Verez. But this, Sarah hits another button, is a week ago at the park." Verez watches as the little girl laughs and runs around the brindle.

The dog rolls over onto its back and the girl drops down on him and hugs his neck. The dog licks the child's face lovingly.

"I wuv Kitty!" the girl kisses the dog's face and Verez feels that she is losing the argument badly.

"My daughter is Autistic Miss Verez, I don't know what you know about the disorder but girls are usually more severely affected by it than boys. Before Kitty came into our lives, Jasmine was nearly catatonic. Can I show you something else Miss Verez?" Sarah asks motioning for Verez to follow her towards the rear of the home.

Walking through the kitchen and out of the back door, Verez follows Sarah out onto the deck and sees the dog walking with the child. The dog bites at flowers every once in a while.

"Kitty bites the bees that are on the flowers. He only does it when Jasmine's outside with him. When he's by himself out there, he leaves them alone...Jasmine's allergic to bee stings Miss Verez."

The little girl tries to ride the dog as it stops to allow her to get on top. Jacob helps her on and she lays down on the dog's broad back, arms around his neck, as he slowly walks around with the little girl on top of him. Verez knows she has lost the debate...what can she argue with, but how can she leave the dog here? As much as they might want the dog, and even fight for it, Verez knows she can get a court order and come back and take it.

"If you take Kitty from us Miss Verez. You'll be taking the one thing that's holding us together. Kitty hasn't just brought Jasmine to life, he's saved our marriage...I honestly believe that. I can't explain how he's done it but I know that he has." Sarah says as tears well up in her eyes.

Suddenly Verez's phone rings and she sees that it's Casey calling. "Hello Chuck!" she answers the phone.

"Yes, I'm here. It's the same house." Verez answers, Sarah crosses her fingers and looks on hopefully as Verez listens on the phone. 'It's the dog from the news." She responds, and Sarah appears to deflate in front of her.

"Is it the same dog that Ron Arwood and Diablo had Verez?" he asks.

Had he put the question any other way then she may have went against what she felt she had to do, but the way Casey asked it changed the way she answered.

"No. No, it's not the same dog." She says and Sarah's eyes grow wide. "Yes, I'm sure. Alright sir...will do." She says before hanging up the phone and being wrapped in the warm loving arms of a grateful mother.

Verez feels the woman's body shake as she cries and she realizes that she has not allowed herself to be hugged since she was a child. Verez fights her own tears even though she has no idea where they are coming from.

"If you've never had a dog in your life Miss Verez. You have to get one because it's almost spiritual the way they make life so much better," Sarah says, holding Verez tight and the tough agent not only allows herself to be held but appreciates the human contact.

It's half an hour before Verez leaves the Hertzle residence but she does so without meeting the brindle, or Kitty, as the dog is now called. Sarah tries to introduce them but Verez declines because just before her and Sarah went back into the house, Verez saw something on the tablet that she and Casey had missed the entire time. Something that could have saved them both a great deal of trouble but then as Verez thinks about it, Diablo would have never have answered for her father's and five other murder's. perhaps seeing it later rather than sooner was for the best.

"Pull up the fight between Hector and the Brindle. Verez waits as Casey does as she directs.

"I got it?" Casey's voice can be heard through the speaker as she drives.

"Seconds thirty-two and forty-nine and then minute twelve thirty on. Rich Jr. can be seen leading the brindle out of the truck through the crowd and finally it's Rich Jr. which is unleashing the dog to fight. You know what that means?"

"It means come home Verez because we got our leverage. Dog fighting is a federal crime!" Casey explains.

"Plea deals and maggots." She nods her head.

"Plea deals and maggots. Come home Verez."

CHAPTER 51

J asmine lies asleep on the couch, Kitty below her on the floor as if keeping Vigil.

"You put Kitty out to go pee pee and I'll put the munchkin to bed. We'll meet back in our room in ten minutes." Sarah winks.

"Maybe less if Kitty will hurry. Come on Kitty." Jacob leads the dog towards the back.

"Give him time to take care of business Jacob or you can clean it up off the carpet this time." Sarah warns before she scoops the little girl up in her arms and carries her up the stairs. "You're getting heavy little girl...soon I'll be the one letting Kitty out to go potty." She whispers to the sleeping child.

Jacob lets Kitty out and steps into his office to check his work emails. While he reads over the only one in his box, Kitty decides to do more than relieve himself.

Several minutes later, Jacob is sitting on the foot of his and Sarah's bed putting his walking shoes on. "He wouldn't go far, Sarah. That dog can't stand to be away from Jasmine." Jacob assures his wife as he gets ready to go look for the dog.

"This wouldn't have happened if you'd fixed that hole in the fence weeks ago." Jacob walks out of the room with her at his heels. "I'm going to go out through the hole in the fence...maybe he's already back or coming back." Jacob walks down the stairs.

The fact that Kitty was so eager to get to Lamb is a notion they've all forgotten. If Jacob did remember and he did decide to go to the Court residence, he still would not believe the dog could have gotten to her. She was protected by an eight-foot privacy fence.

He might not even believe it if he saw the truck on the side of the dirt pile or the muddy paw prints on the top of the white truck's cab. But a half an hour later, when he is home looking for his flashlight, Sarah answers the doorbell to find Jason with Kitty on the end of a leash. Nobody can deny it now...

"I opened the back door and seen the two of them running around together. I don't know how in the hell he got over, under or through the fence but there they were together," Jason says, baffled by the physics of it all.

"You don't think they...you know?" Jacob asks as Jason unhooks the dog.

Kitty goes straight up the stairs and climbs into bed with Jasmine.

"No, I had just put her out ten minutes earlier...there's no way they got it done in time. Jason shakes his head.

CHAPTER 52

The court room is silent save a few whispers and coughs from the packed pews in the spectator's section. Verez cannot help but look at him. The money, connections, and influence. Nash Vance had it all, why would he not walk away? She wonders. Now, in the face of losing everything, he appears not to have a care in the world as he laughs with his attorneys. Every once in a while, he looks back at Verez and Casey, as if looking at slimy hair balls, and smirks in disgust.

"What made him keep going? He was rich way before the agency even got wind of his criminal enterprise? Why not walk away. I always wondered about that?" she asks Casey as quietly as she can.

"Guys like Vance start believing they are untouchable, the more money they make, the more this idea is reinforced. If it hadn't been for a snitch wanting to get out of probation in Knoxville, Tennessee Vance might have stayed below the radar Casey explains.

"I didn't know the guy was in Knoxville who ratted on Vance...that's where Vance is originally from?" Verez sits straight as the federal marshal who acts as bailiff enters the courtroom.

"It was his best friend, that Bob Dolen Rite guy? You saw the file. The guy calls himself "B. right? All these years and you never came across that section?" Casey is surprised.

"As the magistrate judge enters the court the bailiff asks everyone to stand.

"Please be seated," Magistrate Anderson directs, and everyone sits back down.

"You got to read about this "B. right" guy...a real piece of work this junky prick was." Casey whispers out of the corner of his mouth.

"Defense Counsel Beck...does your client understand that he's being charged with multiple counts of trafficking marijuana and...," the judge looks through some papers, "judging by the weight of the product in total he is looking at approximately one hundred and twenty months?" the judge asks.

"Yes, your honor, my client is aware of the charges against him but he maintains his innocence and asks the court to grant a bond so that he may remain with his family while defending himself against these baseless accusations." Vance's lawyers argue.

"The government asks that the court deny the defenses request for bond your honor. Several witnesses have met suspicious ends, or simply disappeared without a trace already your honor and it's out of the safety of the witness in this case that we request a denial of bond." D.A. Locke objects. Defense counsel stands.

"Your honor, my client has no previous criminal records and is a respected philanthropist and pillar of this great city!" the attorney argues. Locke stands once more.

"There are already two bodies and one more that has not been found, because of this case your honor. Because of our justice system, a man cannot be convicted without evidence or witnesses and it's no wonder Mr. Vance has never been convicted before. All witnesses against him are unable to testify and evidence vanishes. We ask that bond be denied." Locke takes his seat.

"Your honor, these accusations are merely meant to prejudice the court against my client."

"No! They are not prejudicial or accusations. They are facts. Facts of which this court does not wish to have reoccur. The court denies the defendants' request for bond!"

Nash Vance turns to his lawyer, red faced and enraged, and curses at him before the marshals lead him through a door into the rear of the courtroom.

"What's on your agenda for the rest of the week?" Casey asks, standing up.

"I am going to the office to get Locke the rest of what I have on Vance but Thursday I'm out of town on a road trip and I'm making a weekend out of it so I won't be back until Monday." She stands and stretches.

"Where are you heading to?" Casey gets a spot in the line filing out of the courtroom.

"I'm actually going back to Ware County. I left something down there." She explains.

"I thought you were going for personal reasons...what was I thinking? You're all work aren't you Verez?" he smiles.

"It's not really work related...I mean it is in a way but not all the way!" she smirks.

Casey looks sideways at her. "It's always work with you."

* * *

CHAPTER 53

A rmondi the Amazing is standing beside his pool, looking at the large Bengal Tiger, with his hands on his hips. There is a small baton in Armondi's hand.

"Streaks, what has gotten into you? It's like you have forgotten everything overnight!" Armondi scolds the great cat as he reaches into his belt pack and removes a treat for the animal. He tosses the meat to the cat who catches it in midair.

"Let's try it again!" he walks up to the feline which growls at him. "Don't you take that tone with me Streaks! You are the star of my show but don't be a diva with me!" Armondi stands in front of the cat. "Let's do the backward walk! Up Streaks! Up!" he raises his hand to show the cat what he wants, and the feline raises up on its hind legs. "Front paws up Streaks! Up!" Lightly tapping the cat's paws with the baton which causes the animal to growl fiercely. "Stop that Streaks!" he yells.

Armondi does not realize that the cat's paws have grown tender from the concrete in its new holding pen. The freshly poured concrete is abrasive and has rubbed the cats paws raw. When he hits the paws with the baton, once more, the cat reacts, enraged by the pain. "Streaks!" Armondi screams as the cat pounces upon the little Italian man. It's dagger like claws tear into the muscles of his back and neck before he feels its teeth puncture his skull. He is not conscious as his cranium is crushed by its powerful jaws and not alive to feel his windpipe being severed by the great beast before it climbs onto a big bale of hay and leaps over his cast iron fence.

THE BRINDLE

CHAPTER 54

"We're home, honey. You want to see Kitty Jazzy?" Sarah watches Jasmine's reaction through the mirror as she pulls into their driveway.

"Kitty! I wuv Kitty!" the child's eyes grow bright.

Sarah laughs as she hits the garage door opener. The door opens about a foot before closing again. Sarah hits the button, and this time the door just vibrates and sounds like a chainsaw before it goes silent.

"Great, another problem for your dad to put off until forever." Sarah rolls her eyes.

She gets out and gets Jasmine out of her car seat. She lets her purse strap hang over one shoulder and puts Jasmine on her opposite hip before making her way to the front door. At the door she realizes that the key she has only fits the back door.

"Wrong key chain...when It rains it pours!" she exclaims, before walking around to the side of the house.

Upstairs, lying on Jasmine's bed, Kitty's eyes open as he hears the sound of keys. He does not raise his head up but his eyes open as he stirs from a deep sleep.

Sarah rounds the corner with Jasmine on her hip. "Child, you are getting too big for mommy to keep carrying you. One day you're going to have to carry me!" she jokes as she reaches the side gate of the private fence.

Sarah enters the fence and does not notice the tiger until after she has shut the gate and turns, nearly running into the big cat.

The feline has a look of rage in its eyes and its maw is stained with the crimson of drying blood. Sarah attempts to go for the gate, but the cat gets between her and the exit. Sarah cries out in fear.

Hearing the scream, Kitty leaps off the bed and rushes out into the hall and down the stairs. He reaches the living room and leaps on the couch to look out of the window and sees only the vehicle in the front yard before he jumps to the other couch and sees the top of Sarah's head and Jasmine in her mother's arms. There is a faint scent in the air, strong and deadly. Kitty dashes toward the kitchen.

Outside, Sarah back peddles slowly with Jasmine nearly being held behind her, on the rear of her hip supported by one arm as the other dangles the purse out of some form of protection between them and the deadly animal.

In a lightning fast sweep from its paw, the purse is ripped from her grasp. Sarah screams >, and the noise only aggravates the large cat further.

Inside the house, Kitty runs, head first, into the back door in an attempt to bust through. After multiple tries he begins to think of another way to get to his family.

As he did the night he first set eyes upon Lamb and decided, against all obstacles, he would get to her... So he is now determined to overcome anything in his way to reach those he loves.

He begins figuring the problem out... The window will be his only way out, it's the easiest way to the back yard where they are.

To get to the window above the kitchen sink he looks the counter over, followed by the kitchen table and one of the kitchen chairs pulled away from the table just so.

He begins climbing onto the kitchen chair, before scrambling on top of the table and, from there leaping onto the kitchen counter. Once he reaches the sink he quickly crawls up to look out of the window. Down below, his heart nearly pops out of his broad scarred chest.

A monster, a creature of which he has never before imagined could exist is poised to attack and its target ...

Propelled by his rear paws, still in the sink, Kitty crashes, head first, through the kitchen window. The loud noise and sudden appearance of Kitty raining down in a shower of broken glass and bad intentions causes Streaks to recoil in surprise.

In the landing one of the toes of his left paw is completely severed as he lands on a large erect shard of glass. The toe, or lack of, is not noticed. Fear driven rage has supplied him with enough endorphins to disregard any pain.

The disruption Kitty has brought into the equation gives Sarah the opportunity she needs as she quickly retreats for the rear door. Just as she turns the corner of the home intent on climbing the back patio steps Kitty turns to look over his shoulder. He sees Jasmine's arms reaching over her mother's shoulders as the child screams for him. He longs to go with her and cannot turn away from the sight of her until she has disappeared behind the home.

His love for her is all consuming, he has no understanding of meaning but what he does understand is that something dared to threaten his love. He turns as the notion rises and grows. He sees the giant before him not as the menacing monster it is by nature but as the agent of danger for his little girl.

His loss of rational thought breaks like a band as he goes into a mode which operates on long encoded genetic instincts. His fearless all pervasive will to war comes from the simple cold fact that he was built for this sole purpose, created for this one thing. He attacks.

Streaks has lifted one front paw to bat at the angry little creature. Kitty sees the paw extended in his direction and with lighting speed, lurches forward and bites down on the large cat's paw. The crunching of bones, as teeth mash down, is followed by the splitting and splicing of Kitty's tongue as Streaks pulls back his mangled paw and one of his extended claws is pushed through Kitty's tongue and ripped through the muscle of the tongue, severing it down the middle.

Kitty has not felt it as blood streams from his growling mouth.

Streaks' rage, now rekindled, causes the huge cat to bristle in preparation for attack but Kitty charges forward first. His instinct's not on survival but a natural instinct embedded some tens of thousands of years ago. This hunter of his little loved one must not survive... at all costs it must not.

His rear claws dig deep into the thick grass and rich soil, as he propels himself, as if shot out of a cannon, beneath the large cats gaping mouth to the fleshy throat just below the chin.

The speed and veracity of the small aggressive creature shocks Streaks. The huge cat leaps back and away from its attacker but the leap backward is not so far or high as Streaks realizes the small angry foe is clinging to his throat.

The massive cat falls back and begins kicking it's rear legs digging his razor sharp claws into the flesh of his attacker. The large cat quickly rolls to his paws and stands while attempting to shake the dog off. It's only after rubbing Kitty off by using the patio steps that the tiger is free of the pit-bull and able to flee out of the huge hole in the fence by which it came.

As he lay there, broken and battered, Kitty feels his body going colder and just before he goes unconscious he swallows the chunk of flesh he took from Streaks. It's warm and meaty and he knows that he has succeeded as the darkness begins to take him.

Though it seems like forever, it's only a few minutes. Sarah and Jasmine go to the dog and find that Kitty is badly injured. Covered in blood and torn to shreds, Kitty is surrounded by medical personnel.

Jasmine squeezes through them and drops to her knees to wrap her arms around the bloody dog. She looks up, tears in her eyes, as Kitty licks the crying child's face one final time before collapsing back to the ground. "No Kitty! No!". The child pleas.

CHAPTER 55

Flaco begins to deal cards as he sits at the table with his Aztec brothers. "You bid too many every time I let you bid first Pito!" he accuses the boy as he deals.

"You pull spades right off and I count my cuts!" the boy fires back.

"You don't count cuts when we bid a dime fool!" Flaco looks at the brother to his left, "He counts his cuts? What the hell is wrong with this fool ese?" he asks.

"Oh shit, there's a tiger running around loose!" one guy yells out.

"No they found it, they said up in the hills!" another older man corrects him.

Flaco and his brothers stop playing to watch the breaking news story as someone turns the TV volume up.

A helicopter hovers over a thicket, its spot light beaming down on an area before men pull the branches back and a tiger's body is seen sprawled out on the ground. An anchorwoman stands to the side holding a clipboard over her head to guard against the blow off from the chopper hovering above.

"Animal rescue workers believe the tiger died from wounds sustained during the altercation with the dog that died protecting the mother and child earlier this afternoon. Some of channel eight's viewers might recall that this dog is the same one that defended this same family from a home invasion a couple of months ago. In fact that incident is what led the family to keep the stray." The woman yells, into the microphone, over the engine of the helicopter above.

"That's something isn't it ? Man's best friend; That was sure some dog." An

186

anchorman says back in the studio.

Pito turns to Flaco and even the amateur comedian is speechless. The entire cell block goes silent.

Flaco smiles and nods his head as he looks around at everyone else. "That was a bad ass dog homes." The new leader of the Aztecs exclaims with pride. The Aztecs all nod their heads in agreement.

"A tiger?" Pito says in disbelief.

CHAPTER 56

All the years and hours invested and the dead-end investigation has culminated in this plush federal courtroom with its crystal water glasses and wall to wall maroon carpeting.

The opening arguments were as theatrical as any Hollywood movie court room scene and Verez has to admit that Joe Lowry, Vance's defense counsel, had won the first round painting the government as taking the word of low level snitches, absconders and even convicted child sex predators in an attempt to create a master mind behind the drug trafficking in Atlanta.

This would have been a great theme to depend on, the jury seemed at first to believe in Lowry's conspiracy theory but as witness after witness took the stand it started becoming clear that an organization of some sort did in fact exist and once Rich Jr. took the stand there was a living breathing eye witness of Vance's involvement.

"He was there the day me and my uncle delivered my uncle's marijuana." Rich Jr. points at Vance as Vance's eyes shoot daggers through the boy's chest.

"Do you know his name?" The U.S. D.A. asks Rich Jr.

"Yes, it's Nash Vance." Rich Jr. responds.

And were you there, were you present when Mr. Vance and Your uncle, Ron Arwood, discussed or made the drug transaction?" The U.S. Attorney General asks.

"No, Uncle Ron gave me the bag of money that Mr. Vance gave him and told me to take it to the truck." Rich Jr. answers before Lowry jumps up.

"Objection! Your honor. The defendant did not watch my client hand his uncle the bag and previously did not claim to in his written or oral statements."

"He's correct, your honor. Please, Richard would you remember if Vance acknowledged the bowling bag that day?" The U.S. Attorney asks.

"Yes, he said that it was a new bowling bag for my uncle. That's what Mr. Vance said." The boy recounts.

"At that point, you took it to the truck... did you happen to see the money personally?" The government attorney asks.

"Yes, I started counting it when I got back to the truck." The boy confesses.

"And how much was there?" The attorney asks.

"I got to one hundred and thirty thousand and still had at least that much more to go... it was supposed to be five hundred thousand."

There were more objections, character witnesses and though Lowry had gotten the suspicious death and disappearances to be left out, the prosecution was able to allude to Vance's part in those as well.

The first two days of the trial had dragged on for nine hours the first and eleven hours the second. On the third, the jury was excused to deliberate and it was lunch time on the fourth day when Verez and Casey were told to be at the court house. The jury had finally reached a verdict.

The federal court is a buzz with activity as people scramble to get packed into the room. Verez and Casey take their usual seats behind the district attorney's section. Vance's cockiness has vanished along with his color. The federal holding facility in Love Joy seems not to have agreed with him, Verez notes. News reporters line the walls with pad and pens out because of the Judge's order to not allow recording devices in the courtroom. The bailiff directs. The collective sound of over two hundred people rising to their feet is heard before Phillips enters and goes to his seat behind the bench.

"Please be seated," the judge permits. "Please, if they are ready, see the jury in Bailiff Leaks." Judge Phillips request.

The bailiff exits the room for a moment before returning and standing to the right of the door as the jury of five men and seven women, walk into the courtroom single file. The jury takes their seats.

Other than a few coughs and papers being shuffled, the federal court room is completely silent. "Has the jury reached its verdict in the case of UNITED STATES OF AMERICA vs. NASH ALLEN VANCE?" Judge Phillips asks.

A tall older man with a crew cut stand. "Yes, your honor." The foreman hands a piece of paper to the bailiff who hands it immediately to the judge. Judge Phillips opens the paper, reads it, but gives no indication of the verdict.

"What says the jury?" the judge asks.

"In the case of the United States of America versus Nash Allen Vance, we the jury find the defendant guilty of trafficking over five thousand kilograms of marijuana." The courtroom explodes as the foreman announces the guilty verdict. Vance begins to yell something, the judge calls order, but Casey and Verez are already exiting the courtroom.

Outside, on the courthouse steps, reporters flock toward the defense attorney as Casey and Verez watch from the sidelines. Rich Jr. comes out of the courtroom and sees Verez, "Excuse me...ah, Agent Verez?" the young man asks from a safe distance away.

Verez turns to him with a look of disdain. "What?" she asks obviously annoyed.

"Well, I was ah, I was wondering...since I helped you guys and all? Can I have Sugar back? She' the last of her blood line and I..." "No!" Verez interrupts him.

"No! And if I ever catch you anywhere near a pit bull or a dog fight, ever again, I'll have you in a federal prison being passed around like a peace pipe! You get me?" she threatens.

The boy nods his head and backs away; when he is gone Casey explodes with laughter followed by Verez. "A peace pipe? Where the hell did that come from? Casey laughs.

"I don't know? I really don't.   I just can't stand that little rat!" she confesses.

"You know Verez; if I didn't know better, I'd say you are a closet outlaw. You hate prison guards and snitches. I'm glad you chose this side of the law!" he laughs.

"I can't stand people that abuse children either...you left that out!" she reminds him.

"None of us can stand them. No matter what side of the law you're on." Casey admits. For a moment they stare ahead in silence.

"You know...I was disappointed when Blake told me that the brindle was the one at the Hertzle home. I couldn't believe that you would lie to me?" Casey stares straight ahead.

"Let me explain..." Verez begins before Casey holds his hand up to silence her.

"As I was saying. I was disappointed, at first, but then I thought about it. You are the most dedicated agent that I have ever known so I knew that you must have had one hell of a reason to do what you did. When I heard that our dog died protecting the mother and child...from a tiger, no less! The point is, I'm proud of you." Verez smiles but says nothing.

"Oh, also I have another case for you. Another kingpin case, if you are interested?" he offers.

"I think I'm going to take a vacation." She says watching his look of surprise.

"Vacation? You? You haven't taken a vacation since I've known you? What's with you lately? You took a couple of days off two months ago when you went back to Ware County. Did you meet someone?" he wonders as Verez's Suburban is brought around front by an intern from the office.

"Actually, Verez says as she heads towards the vehicle, I did." She smiles over her shoulder at him.

"Well, when do I get to meet him?" Casey asks from the steps.

"It's not a he!" She yells back. "Oh, oh, okay I get it!" He seems un-surprised.

"No, you don't!" she shakes her head. The intern gives her the keys.

"How was she?" Verez asks the young man.

"She was just great." He smiles and helps her into the vehicle. Verez starts the truck and looks at the passenger side seat.

"Let's go home Sugar!" she says to the Brindle's brown sister. Sugar leans over and licks Verez's face, and the hard nose agent laughs as she drives away.

She thinks about what Sarah Hertzle told her that day on the back deck of the Hertzle home. She was right. Verez thinks to herself, having a dog makes life so much better. She can feel hers getting better every day.

CHAPTER 57

S arah watches from the open door of Jasmine's room as the little girl sits on the edge of her bed and stares ahead at nothing. The child has not spoken since the day that Kitty died, except for a morning when she awoke looking around for the dog calling its name until she sat on the kitchen floor and began crying.

Kitty had died and would not be coming back. Though Jacob continued to spend lots of time at home helping Sarah with Jasmine, the child seems to have gotten worse than she was before the dog came into their lives. Sarah watches as the little girl slips further and further away.

Jacob climbs the stairs and stands beside his wife. "I guess the dog did no good?" he asks, seeing his daughter sit emotionlessly up on the bed.

"It didn't even cause her to flinch when it licked her face. Tell Les I appreciate it though." Sarah sighs.

"That's only two dogs that we've tried...we'll keep trying until we find one that can reach her." He hugs Sarah.

"No, there was something about Kitty. Something other dogs don't have Jacob? I don't know if it was the way he was abused all those years or what, but there was just something special about that dog."

"You don't think I know that Sarah? Kitty is probably the only reason my wife and daughter are alive today! I know that he was special but what do we do? Give up?" he asks turning her to face him so that he can look into her eyes.

"No! Of course not! But it's going to be a long hard fight. Kitty came into our lives like a gift from The Heavenly Father and now he's gone!" Sarah looks at her daughter and wishes she knew what was happening in her daughter's head.

What was going on inside the child's head, at that very moment, was something like a daydream but more vivid. Almost as if she were directing and producing a movie, one which she and Kitty, still very much alive, starred in together. Here Jasmine and Kitty are together, here Kitty has not died and Jasmine has nothing to fear. This is the child's safe place. The world around her is frightening, big and full of things that scare her. So in her head she decides to stay but before kitty, even it was a sad place. Void of color, happiness or memories as if locking herself in a colorless room, away from the loud terrifying world outside.

Kitty was a guardian, a protector, a security blanket that warded off all of her many fears and anxieties. Kitty gave her the confidence to join and enjoy the world about her but now with Kitty no longer in that world, it is unbearable. When Jasmine retreated within her safe place, she found Kitty waiting for her there. The dog's memories returned with her and with Kitty here she has no reason ever to leave again.

The days are spent playing together in fields of high green grass and flowers with no bees but only butterflies. The nights, cuddled safely up to the dog as she has always done. In here, they speak as they had out there. She knew the first time she met Kitty that he could hear her and she him. He hears her inner voice and she hears his, as only they can and so the child decides that this is the world she will remain in.

Outside of Jasmine's world, she does not hear her parents talking as they stare hopelessly at their daughter. She also does not hear the doorbell.

"I got it, honey." Jacob kisses his wife's cheek before he descends the stairs. Sarah stares at her daughter and prays to be shown the answer.

"Sarah!" Jacob calls to her from downstairs.

"What's wrong?" she asks, surprised by the urgency in her husband's voice.

"Get Jasmine...there's something she needs to see!" he yells, and Sarah hears a tone in his voice that she has not heard in the house in months...one of excitement.

In her head, Jasmine has not heard the exchange between her parents as she and Kitty walk upon a grassy knoll beneath the warm summer sun. She does have a sensation of her body being lifted in her mother's arms out there, but she ignores it, not wanting to pollute the perfect moment with Kitty. The dog turns to her and licks her face gently before putting his forehead to her forehead. She smiles as they sit in the cool grass forehead to forehead but slowly her smile fades for Kitty is leaving her.

"No Kitty! Stay!" she cries with the voice that only he hears. He cannot, he must leave, and she must go back to the outside world. It's more of a feeling than a voice...a feeling she can hear as she struggles to accept it, why is he leaving? Why, when everything is perfect here where they can be together forever? She feels his answer, but it makes no sense. Out there they cannot be together again...out there he is gone? She pleads but Kitty parts from her and climbs the knoll and disappears over the hill.

The colors fade, the grass dies, and she finds herself in the dark room of her mind. In the world beyond her parents have taken her into the garage of the Court's where Lamb lays upon a blanket with five puppies suckling.

"Look at them Jacob...just like their mother as white as cotton." Jason motions toward the four white puppies. "That one though...that looks just like his papa. Just cuter." Jason points at the fifth puppy.

As if the small brindle puppy hears something, he pulls his head away from his mother's breast and turns his blind eyes up toward the child in Sarah's arms.

A voice calls to her from beyond the darkness and Jasmine knows it well as she swings the door of her mind open. She turns to look down at the puppy who looks blindly in her direction. Arms out stretched towards the brindle pup Jasmine's eyes brighten. "Kitty!"

THE BRINDLE

* * *

DEDICATIONS

I would like to thank the following people who have not only made "The Brindle" possible but have also shown me the importance of friendship. I believe everyone who knows me knows the value I place on my friendships because none of us have nearly as many as we believe.

To Richard-Enrique Ulloa – my best and most loyal friend, your faith in me has been so strong that is has even reinforced my belief in myself. You and I are just beginning a journey and I am honored to call you my friend.

Tilmon Partin – You mean old bastard. The youngest seventy-year-old that ever lived. You've encouraged me to keep going and shown me that, no matter what, giving up is never an option.

Aaron Bennett – The first person that had ever gotten out and kept his word. Never underestimate how much a man's word being kept means in this world. I've never forgotten our pact, nor will I, and as you did so shall I stay true to my oath.

Robert Warner Blake – To my new friend for the wonderful and professional graphic design, cover and back page.

J. JENNINGS MELTON'S

"The Brindle"

About the Author:

J. Jennings Melton was born in South Bend, the county of St. Joseph Indiana, in 1979. He lived, as a child, in Texas, Northern Indiana and Tennessee. Raised by a drug addicted father, he would spend many of his teen years incarcerated. It was in juvenile and penal institutions where he developed a love for literature and a passion for writing. Upon release the author enrolled in college while on parole in Knoxville, Tennessee, The Brindle is the first of many works to come.

J. Jennings Melton can be contacted at: JJenningsMelton.com   or

jasonmelton81@gmail.com

He will appreciate any feedback or comments and will respond as promptly as his schedule will allow.

COMMENTS OR REVIEWS

"I thoroughly enjoyed "The Brindle". I found the brutal scenes to be just that...brutal, and the emotional scenes leaving me wracked with uncontrollable sobbing. Thank You Jason."
---- Robert Warner Blake

"This book is captivating from the very first sentence."
---- Jack Roberts.

"I found this book very emotional, I found myself crying several times"
----   Richard   Enrique   Ulloa

DISCLAIMER

"ANY AND ALL CHARACTERS IN "THE BRINDLE" ARE ENTIRELY INVENTIONS AND CREATIONS OF THE AUTHOR. ANY NAMES OR SITUATIONS THAT MAY MATCH THOSE OF REAL PEOPLE OR REAL OCCURRENCES ARE NOTHING MORE THAN MERE COINCIDENCES."

www.ingramcontent.com/pod-product-compliance
Lightning Source LLC
Chambersburg PA
CBHW070843120626
46556CB00002B/852